CANDLELIGHT REGENCY SPECIAL

S0-BEF-037

CANDLELIGHT REGENCIES

An Intriguing Innocent

Rebecca Ashley

A CANDLELIGHT REGENCY SPECIAL

Dedicated
to
Mom

Published by
Dell Publishing Co., Inc.
1 Dag Hammarskjold Plaza
New York, New York 10017

Copyright © 1980 by Lois A. Walker

All rights reserved. No part of this book may be
reproduced or transmitted in any form or by any
means, electronic or mechanical, including photocopying,
recording or by any information storage and retrieval
system, without the written permission of the
Publisher, except where permitted by law.

Dell ® TM 681510, Dell Publishing Co., Inc.

ISBN: 0-440-10258-8

Printed in the United States of America
First printing—November 1980

CHAPTER ONE

I didn't see the vehicle that rounded the bend at breakneck speed until it was almost upon me. Then I dived for the ditch, flinging myself headlong into it and throwing my arms up to cover my head as the conveyance swayed dangerously to avoid me. Crouched amidst the undergrowth, with my shoulders hunched and my eyes closed tightly, I heard the sound of horses neighing and plunging as the vehicle groaned to a halt. I was trembling so violently that I couldn't think. I must have remained in the ditch a minute or so, listening to the voices of men trying to regain control of the horses.

"The girl! See if she's all right," I heard someone shout. "Damn, I'll see myself." A moment later a hand pried my arms off my head. "You're not hurt, child," the voice declared matter-of-factly. "Open your eyes and get out of the ditch."

In my excited state my fear turned to indignation at the cavalier attitude this farmer had adopted toward me. I shouted back at him, "I shall open my eyes when you speak to me with the same concern you show to a couple of nags."

There was a short, nasty laugh. "I shall show you as

5

much concern as I show my cattle when you act as intelligently."

Furious, I opened my eyes to confront my tormentor. Standing in the ditch in front of me was a tall, dark-haired man. The sardonic expression on his face only increased my anger. Groping in my mind for something to say which would give him a sharp setdown, I drew myself up to my full height. As my full height came only to his shoulder, I must admit that it was a little hard to achieve the withering scorn I wished to convey. "You, sir, are on private property," I said in frigid tones.

He threw back his head and laughed. "And you, miss, were standing in the middle of the road showing no regard for your own safety or that of any conveyance which passed this way. You can see what has been the result of your carelessness." He gestured toward his conveyance.

The dismay I felt must have been written plainly on my face. There stood one of the most elegant carriages I had ever seen—not that I had seen many in this remote part of Kent. It was a rich dark red with an elaborate crest of gold on the side. Two liveried men in matching red uniforms with gold trim stood by the horses, still murmuring soothing words to them. And what horses! They were powerfully built, perfectly matched, chestnut-colored animals. Judging from the shine of their coats, no attention had been spared them.

I dragged my eyes from the splendor of this vision and looked back at the man standing beside me. He was wearing a bottle-green coat which matched the extraordinary green of his eyes. The coat sat superbly on a pair of broad shoulders which were obviously not the result of padding. My eyes traveled down to his dun-colored breeches fitted to a well-formed leg. His boots were highly polished Hessians. My gaze stopped there, and I continued to stare downward, too taken aback to look up.

"Does my attire meet with your approval?" he inquired haughtily.

"Yes, sir," I mumbled in embarrassment.

"Good," he replied coldly. "Now, as you have satisfied yourself about me, permit me to satisfy my curiosity concerning you."

I opened my mouth to protest, but he interrupted. "Since you have nearly overset my carriage—were Shingles not such a first-rate whip you should have done so—I hardly think it an unfair question."

"I live in the cottage over there." I gestured down the lane leading off the road.

"Ah," he said thoughtfully. "I shall escort you home."

"I do not think that is necessary, sir. I'm perfectly capable of taking care of myself."

"So you've proven," he said dryly.

Ignoring that thrust, I turned with all the dignity I could muster and attempted to climb out of the ditch. Though not over three feet deep, its sides were quite steep and I slid back down. The man beside me grinned in a most ungentlemanlike way. I felt my face slowly redden.

"Allow me," he said with exaggerated gallantry as he leaped out of the ditch and extended his hand to pull me up. Deposited back on the road, thoroughly humiliated, I turned and stalked off down the lane. At

7

least I had meant to stalk off; but with mud caked heavily on both shoes, stumped off would have been a better description.

"Glad to have been of service," the arrogant man threw after me.

I continued walking steadily, if somewhat ungracefully, down the lane. I heard one of the coachmen snicker, "Comely chit, even if she did upset our bits o' blood."

Hidden from sight by the trees, I stopped to wipe the mud off my shoes with a stick. Sighing, I rose and trudged on down the lane to the cottage door. Pausing outside, I glanced at my clothes, noting ruefully that my white apron was flecked with mud and the hem of my dark dress was a wet, grimy brown.

Well, there was nothing for it now but to proceed inside, I decided as I pushed open the door and ventured inside. Mrs. Worthing sat working on a sampler by the window. She looked up as I entered, her warm expression of greeting fading to disapproval when she saw my clothes.

Mrs. Worthing was the kindly widow I had lived with for the past six years. That was when Papa decided that at thirteen I was too old to travel with him in his various jobs as a roving preacher, barber, gambler, and peddler—and had sent me to live with my dead mama's old friend.

"Well, well," she clucked, rising slowly from her favorite chair. "What have you been into, child?"

"I fell," I answered, avoiding the questioning blue eyes of the short, plump woman.

"To be expected in the young," she murmured,

smoothing back her wispy gray hair as she reached me and turned around to untie my apron.

Although I was nineteen, Mrs. Worthing still regarded me as young and immature. I have to admit that her belief was founded on convincing evidence. In the last month I had dropped a cut-crystal dish I was admiring at Mrs. Carey's house and it broke into a thousand pieces, spilled tea on the vicar during his annual visit to our cottage, and sat on Mrs. Worthing's spectacles, crushing them totally. I was not malicious, trouble just seemed to follow me around.

"Wash up, Victoria," Mrs. Worthing broke into my reverie. "Then I have some exciting news for you."

I obeyed, washing my face and hands in the bowl in my small bedroom and changing my apron. I wondered if Mrs. Worthing's news had anything to do with Papa. He generally came through to visit me once every two or three months, but for the last seven months I hadn't seen or heard from him, and his prolonged absence was beginning to worry me.

"Victoria," Mrs. Worthing called, "are you going to be all day?" This must be news indeed to arouse the impatience of the usually imperturbable Mrs. Worthing! I toweled off my hands and went back into the tiny living room. Mrs. Worthing motioned me to a wooden footstool by her chair and picked up her needlework. Pushing an imaginary pair of spectacles back on her nose, she announced, "News, child! The new master is coming." She paused expectantly.

My mind raced. New master? Could that man on the road . . . ? No, he couldn't be. But the awful realization was dawning in my mind that not only could

9

the arrogant stranger be the new master, he most probably was. What else would a stranger with magnificent clothes and a carriage such as his be doing here? And I had accused him of being on private property!

"Well, missy, don't you have any questions? Like 'Is he handsome?' " Mrs. Worthing prompted.

"Is he handsome?" I asked, hoping fervently that she would say he was old and decrepit.

She laid her sampler on her lap and looked dreamily ahead. "Yes. Mrs. Carey says he's quite tall with ever-so-dark hair and very green eyes under fierce black eyebrows. He has a straight nose and a solemn line of a mouth—he doesn't smile much."

My last hope was dashed. She had described to perfection the man I had met on the road. "How does Mrs. Carey know what he looks like?" I asked curiously.

"Her sister works in a house in London. It's not hard to hear about him in London. Every mama with a marriageable daughter is angling for him. He has plenty of money to back up his looks," she explained.

I wriggled on the footstool as my mind worked. Mrs. Worthing's job as housekeeper to the large manor house at the front of the estate made Lord Linton's arrival more than an item of passing interest to us. No one had lived in the house since old Mr. Winterwood had decided to forsake the peace and quiet of country life for London some twelve years ago. He had never returned to Kent and had died four months ago, leaving the estate to a distant relative. The new owner—Lord Wesley Earl Christopher Cresham, Marquis of Linton—had shown no interest in his new property. Now he had apparently come to survey his inheritance.

"Will he be staying long?" I asked, thinking that with any luck it would be a short visit and he would not see me again. Living with Mrs. Worthing, I was, in effect, living on the charity of the master of Meadow-acres. Mr. Winterwood had always sent without question funds for Mrs. Worthing's support and the upkeep of her cottage. But a new master might not want to support someone who had no real claim on him. Of course, I did help Mrs. Worthing keep the manor house clean, but I wasn't officially hired as a servant and, after my encounter with Lord Linton this morning, he might be adamant that I not be employed by him.

"Staying long?" Mrs. Worthing repeated. "I shouldn't think so. His solicitors notified me only today that he'll be arriving shortly and wishes the house prepared. They said it might be an extended visit, but I daresay he'll tire of country life quickly. Mrs. Carey says he has quite a reputation around London." She raised her eyebrows slightly on the last sentence. "Yes, I rather think Kent will not offer the same attractions for him that London does."

"You mean he's a rake?" I asked curiously.

"Victoria Ann! I never in my life—" She broke off, sputtering. "Rake indeed!" She jabbed her needle through the sampler several times with great vigor.

"I'd best wash out my dress," I said, rising with alacrity and exiting from the room. By the time I returned, Mrs. Worthing was in better spirits and to keep her that way I tactfully refrained from mentioning the new master for the rest of the evening.

The following morning she and I walked toward the great house to give it one final cleaning before Lord Linton arrived. At least Mrs. Worthing was still under

11

the impression that he had not yet arrived and, as I could scarcely tell her differently without relating the incidents of yesterday's carriage mishap, I remained silent.

It was with considerable trepidation that I walked down the tree-lined lane to the manor house. Coming around a bend in the road, the house loomed impressively ahead of us. It had been standing for several centuries. The original house was a large Tudor-style mansion built of limestone which had weathered to a dull gray. Over the years various tenants had added to the structure as the need arose, building succeeding additions of varying styles, all from the same limestone. Newer additions were in different shades of gray since the rock was in progressive stages of weathering.

We approached the house from the front, passing the broad sweeping stairway to the main entrance and following a path around to the back door. Inside the back door five people were nervously assembled. Mrs. Worthing had only this morning hired them from the village to work in the house. After a few preliminary pleasantries she assigned everyone a task, and we went off briskly to fulfill our new positions as servants. Truth to tell, we were a motley lot of unemployables with nothing to say for ourselves but a willingness to please and a vast ignorance of what being a proper servant meant.

After I broke two plates in the kitchen, Mrs. Worthing reassigned me to work in the garden under the mistaken impression that I could do very little damage there. And that's where I was half an hour later, bent over some furry red geraniums, when I heard voices be-

12

hind me. Turning, I saw Mrs. Worthing coming down the path with Lord Linton.

"And this is Victoria. She's the only servant you haven't met. Victoria, make a curtsy to his lordship."

I smiled nervously and curtsied badly. Rising, I saw the marquis regarding me with scarcely concealed amusement. "Well, well. Tell me, Victoria, in your capacity as gardener will you also warn trespassers off my property?"

"Oh dear, no, sir," Mrs. Worthing broke in. "The gamekeeper will do that. Victoria here is far too timid to undertake such a job."

"Indeed?" the marquis said, smiling openly.

My heart sank. So he had recognized me, and worse, was not going to let me forget what I had said during our encounter on the road. I wondered if he intended to say anything privately to Mrs. Worthing about me, or order me off his property here and now. I looked at him anxiously.

But he had already put me from his mind and was looking about the garden with a slight frown. "I shall have to have a team of gardeners sent from one of my other estates. This garden has been sadly neglected." He turned back to me. "Don't look so downcast. It will be a week or so before they arrive and after that we shall find something else for you to do." Addressing Mrs. Worthing, he asked, "Is this all of the garden?"

"No, milord, it extends around to the side of the house." As they left to inspect the rest of the garden, I relaxed. At least the marquis was not going to throw me out of house and home. I turned cheerfully back to my task.

CHAPTER TWO

"Well, she said she's not coming, so I guess that's final."

"Yes, it certainly is final," Lord Linton echoed.

I peered around the hedges to see two men seat themselves on a marble bench by the sundial. Their backs were to me, and they were so engrossed in their conversation that they didn't hear me. I slipped back behind the hedge and listened guiltily. A week had passed since Lord Linton's arrival at the manor, but I had not seen him since Mrs. Worthing had introduced us.

"Yes, it's damned final," Lord Linton repeated. "She needn't think when I return to London there will be any reconciliation. If she prefers not to rusticate with me, then she's welcome to find someone else. I leave her to it."

"Really, Wes," the other man said in a placating voice, "don't you think you're being a little hard? I mean she's not used to country living, and I don't think she would be accepted very graciously here in rural Kent." After a pause he added shrewdly, "Unless, of course, you marry her."

Intrigued by the stranger's pleasant voice, I ventured another peek from behind the bushes. Lord Linton was still seated with his back to me, but his companion was now pacing in front of him. The newcomer was of average height with a crop of reddish hair curling riotously but appealingly about his head. He was dressed fashionably in a blue waistcoat and a tight-fitting pair of white unmentionables. As he rounded the sundial and turned to walk back to the bench, I ducked back behind my hedge.

"Put the thought of marriage right out of your mind," said Lord Linton. "I've not remained unshackled this long by being susceptible to manipulating women. She needn't think I'll be pining away for her either. There are plenty of women down here to amuse me."

"I wouldn't be too certain of that, Wes. This is a rather provincial part of England, and I don't think women will stand in line to be your *chère amie* the way they do in London. And God knows why they do there; you treat them like the very devil."

"There are women everywhere who will sleep with a man if there's something in it for them—jewels, furs, money. Everyone has a price." Lord Linton's words were harsh and grating. "As a matter of fact I nearly ran over a girl the other day that I might make some arrangements with." As if talking to himself, he added, "Black hair, blue eyes, skin like ivory, and as delicate a set of features as I've ever seen. Yes, I believe I shall make some arrangements."

"You can't be serious, Wes. You came down here to live in this godforsaken part of the country, and if you wish to live in peace, you'll need to earn the goodwill of the local people. If you begin by ravishing their daughters, you certainly won't have it."

"Please, Edward, you make me sound so base. I have never ravished anyone in my life and I have more than once been close to being ravished. And as for the good-will of the people, I should think I've earned that already. For the past week I have played host to the sorriest crowd of servants it has ever been my misfortune to meet. Only this morning I had a cup of coffee dumped in my lap, and that's the third time in as many days. And just look at this garden. It looks like it's cared for by a nearsighted mole."

Ignoring the marquis's complaints, his friend continued blandly, "Suit yourself, Wes. Find someone here or remove back to London, but she is not coming."

"Devil take her," Lord Linton growled.

His companion made some reply that was lost to me. Peeping around the greenery, I could see them moving back to the house. I returned to clipping the hedges, my mind busy with the scene that I had just witnessed. That the marquis had a light-o'-love was obvious from the discussion between the two men. Although I had heard the rumors about him, to hear such scandalous events actually discussed by the people participating was something new to me. Of course, having spent the last six years in isolated Chilham, there were a great many things that were new to me.

"Victoria!"

I jumped and whirled to encounter a very stern-looking Mrs. Worthing. "I'm sorry, I didn't hear you. Had you called before?" I asked sheepishly.

"Called before?" she grumbled. "I have said your name well above a dozen times. What in the world are you doing here?" she demanded, transferring her gaze from me to the hedge.

"Trimming."

Her blue eyes nearly bulged out of her head as she looked the length of the hedge that I had trimmed.

"Dear me," she sighed.

I turned back to survey my handiwork. I must admit that the hedge was not absolutely straight. To be quite truthful, there was not a straight line in the whole hedge, up and down or back and forth. In places it had been trimmed almost to the stalk and in other places it appeared not to have been trimmed at all.

"It will take a year to grow back out to a decent hedge," she lamented.

"I'm terribly sorry. I don't know how that could have happened. Honestly, I was very careful."

"It's all right, child," she consoled. "I daresay you didn't mean to wreck the garden; you just fell into daydreaming while you were working." She patted my hand sympathetically. "Victoria, dear, perhaps you would like to do some other sort of work about the house," she suggested tactfully.

"You're angry because I ruined the hedge," I murmured downcast.

"I'm not angry about that."

"Is it because I pruned back the rose bushes that were about to bloom? I can explain that—"

"I'm not angry, Victoria," she interrupted. "I just thought perhaps you would enjoy doing something else. Besides, the master's gardeners will be arriving shortly, and this is man's work."

"Then you're not angry?" I pressed.

"Not a bit of it," she assured me as she put her arm around me and began to draw me toward the house. "What's your fancy?"

"Well, I would like to be a maid like Janey," I admitted.

"A maid it is. I'll put you on the second floor until you have a little experience."

"Thank you, Mrs. Worthing. I'm certain that I shall like it, and there's nothing that can go wrong being a maid."

But I was destined to have my words proved wrong not two days later. On that particular day I was studiously changing the bedclothes in Lord Linton's room when he walked in. He had closed the door behind him before noticing me; then he stopped, his hand arrested in the act of unfastening the cuff of his lawn shirt, and regarded me with surprise. Slowly his face took on a calculating look. "Well, if it isn't the blue-eyed beauty herself," he drawled softly. "I would definitely call this fate."

Something about the look on his face put me on my guard. I looked past him to the door and bundled the sheets up protectively in front of me.

"There's no need to stare at the door as if it's your last means of escape, pet," he said in soft accents.

Obediently I turned my wide-eyed gaze to him.

"And there's no need to act like a doe confronting the hunter," he continued disarmingly. "But since you are here, it might be an excellent time for us to get to know one another." He was across the room in three

19

strides. He took the sheets out of my arms and tossed them to the floor. I watched in fascination as he turned back to me and tilted his head to one side, regarding me quizzically. I looked dumbly back into his eyes. As I watched, his face came steadily closer until I closed my eyes. The next thing I felt was his lips pressing against mine—it was a cool touch but heavy and persistent. I stood frozen motionless. He drew back, and I opened my eyes to meet his cold and dispassionate stare.

"God, an innocent," he sneered. "I should have known." His words were awful in their contemptuousness. "Get out of my bedroom and don't ever come in here again." He stood aside, and I fled to the door.

I fumbled blindly with the doorknob, my mind clouded by the events that had just occurred. I had been kissed by one or two village lads, chaste boys who gave me pecks on my cheek and then drew back to blush shyly, but I had certainly never been kissed like that.

Lord Linton removed my nerveless hand from the knob and opened the door. "The trouble with Incomparables," he observed, "is that they cannot do even the simplest things for themselves."

I averted my eyes as I fled past him through the door and heard it close emphatically behind me. I stood uncertainly in the hall, staring at the closed door. My lips burned where he had touched them. I put my hand tentatively up to them and touched them with the tips of my fingers, thinking I should have been able to feel the heat from them but they felt only cool—cool like his lips when they had come down on mine. I blushed to the roots of my hair at the thought.

But my humiliation was giving way to something else as I stood regarding the door he had closed so unceremoniously in my face. A tide of resentment swelled through me. Lord Linton was fair and far out if he thought he could take such liberties with me and then push me out into the hall! I turned angrily on my heel and started down the stairs toward the kitchen to find Mrs. Worthing. As I walked, my steps increased to keep pace with my mounting anger. When Mrs. Worthing heard the story I had to tell, she would march right up to milord's room and tell him in no uncertain terms what would be the consequences of taking such liberties with me. Now that I was safely away from my employer, I began to think of all the tart things I should have said to him. Yes, I should have said, "Take your nasty, filthy hands off me." No, that was too polite. I should have said, "Sir, how dare you touch me in such a familiar way!" and slapped him roundly. I pushed the door to the kitchen open and darted in.

I glanced about the large kitchen with its baskets hanging from the ceiling and gleaming copper pans hanging about the wall. By the stone fireplace Janey sat peeling potatoes nonchalantly on a high-backed settle.

"Where's Mrs. Worthing?" I demanded.

"Went to town." She looked up indifferently from her chore. "How come your face is so red?"

I crossed the room and dropped onto the settle beside her. "Janey, do you swear to keep a secret?"

"Course," she replied, her monkeylike face still bent over the potato on her lap and her red hair nodding up and down to the movement of the knife.

21

"Well, you didn't the last time—about my breaking the Sèvres vase; you told everyone that story," I reminded her.

"I won't this time." She reached for another potato.

"I've just come from Lord Linton's bedroom. He attempted to take such shocking liberties with me. I positively blush to tell you." I stated my dramatic news in a rush of words. "When Mrs. Worthing comes back, I shall tell her of his actions and she shall most certainly give him a very sharp setdown."

Janey sedately continued to peel the potato. "Wouldn't do that," she advised.

"What?"

"Don't say anything about what happened."

"Janey," I began again, a little more theatrically this time. "You cannot conceive the outrageous things that rake—" I rose from the settle in agitation.

"Victoria," she commanded, "sit back down and listen to me. Lord Linton can do what he wishes in his own house. Mrs. Worthing is his housekeeper, and at her age she could hardly find another position; it would only serve to upset her if you told her of this little incident. I daresay he didn't really attempt you. He just wanted to see if you were willing. He didn't force you, did he?"

"Well, no," I had to admit. "But he was overly familiar," I ended with prim dignity.

Janey broke into helpless laughter, and potatoes rolled off her lap and across the floor in all directions.

"What's so funny?" I demanded irritably.

"You," she gurgled. "Overly familiar," she mimicked. "You would think a man was being overly familiar if he nodded to you." Laughter overcame her again, and I waited frostily until she subsided back to sobriety.

"I don't think it is at all amusing," I informed her as she made an effort to compose her wide mouth back into a solemn line and brushed the wild red hair back from her face.

"I'm sorry I laughed," she apologized with no look of contrition. "But you mustn't say anything to Mrs. Worthing. It would only upset her."

"You're right, I guess," I acknowledged as I sank onto the bench beside her and picked up a potato.

"Guests?" Mrs. Worthing said as she bustled through the door, carrying a basket. "Did I hear you say guests?"

"Er, yes," I replied.

"I didn't know you knew they were coming," she commented as she began removing items from the basket.

"Guests here?" Janey asked.

"Yes, his lordship intends to have several people down for a week or so and open the house up for entertainment."

"When?" Janey and I asked in unison.

"Next week. He certainly has been good for our lazy little village," she enthused. "All of the shopkeepers have been kept busy filling our orders for the manor house. Next the master's going to send to London for some wallpapers and fabrics to completely redecorate the house." She pushed her mobcap back on her gray curls and continued. "Not that the house needs to be thoroughly redone, but some of the drapes are a trifle faded and the carpets are a bit worn in spots."

"Umm," I agreed absently.

"Victoria, you've pared that potato down to almost nothing," Mrs. Worthing exclaimed.

"Sorry," I apologized hastily.

"Here, let me put it on to cook. You two girls run along now and prepare the dining room for dinner."

We obeyed, running down the long, carpeted hall to the elaborate dining room. With its watered-silk green walls and lush green velvet drapes it seemed to me a room out of a fairy tale. A long shiny walnut table was flanked by a dozen carved chairs. As I carefully handled the fine china and Janey set the silverware with a great clinking of metal, we continued our discussion about the marquis.

"I should like him to kiss me," she rhapsodized after hearing the whole of my story. "What was it like?"

I paused in my task. "It wasn't much like anything. I mean I didn't feel anything. Perhaps you have to be in love with someone before they can inspire any sort of response."

"I don't think so," Janey observed. "You set the plates wrong."

I looked in confusion at the dishes in front of the chair at the head of the long table. "How can one person use so many plates? It only takes me one to eat dinner."

"That's because you're not Quality," she sniffed.

"And I suppose you know a great deal about Quality?" I challenged.

"I know that the ladies all fan themselves delicately while the men survey them with quizzing glasses. It's all very elegant. And they have wonderful balls where the men dance waltzes with the ladies and hold them very close, like so." Janey danced past me and whirled me into her arms. Laughing, we half danced, half stomped about the dining room table.

"Girls," Mrs. Worthing's voice cut into our merriment. "His lordship wishes to dine now."

We stopped short and looked up into the unamused face of Lord Linton standing just beyond Mrs. Worthing and towering considerably above her. I slowly dropped my arms from about Janey's waist as she let go of me. I cast my eyes to the floor and shuffled out past the marquis with Janey following close behind me.

"Girls will be girls," Mrs. Worthing told the marquis as we exited.

CHAPTER THREE

"No!" I cried in a denial that combined shock with a fascinated curiosity. "They don't really, do they?"

"They do," Janey repeated, nodding her head so vigorously she loosened her hairpins and her red hair came cascading down into her face. Using the back of her hand to sweep it back, she continued dusting flour across the pastries. "Some of their dresses completely reveal their bosoms."

"How positively shocking! Do you know any more one dites?" I asked, anxious to hear even more shocking gossip about the ladies from London.

"On-dits," she corrected. "Well, some of the women dampen their clothes to cling to their body."

"Do they go out in public like that?"

"Lord, yes! They go to balls and parties that way to attract men's attention." She lowered her voice to a whisper. "Sometimes they don't wear anything under the damp dresses."

I stopped rolling the pin over the piecrust. "Are you serious?" I asked incredulously.

As the kitchen door opened, we both ceased talking and applied ourselves vigorously to our tasks. Mrs. Worthing hurried in. "Good. At least you girls are hard at work. I just saw Virgina flirting in the hall with one of the new footmen. I wish Lord Linton hadn't insisted on bringing his own servants down. We were doing quite well without them," she grumbled. "Next week he's going to have even more here, and there is already an army of gardeners rooting about in the garden." She moved on through the kitchen and left by the back door.

"Things certainly are becoming exciting around here," Janey observed. "My cousin went to London once, but she's the only person I know who's ever spent any time there. With all these eligible men—footmen, gardeners, butlers—coming from all over England as well as London we shall have our pick of men." Her monkeyish face shone at the prospect.

"Do you want to get married?" I asked curiously.

"Are you proposing?"

"Do you want to marry someone?" I persisted. "You're only seventeen."

"Of course I want to get married. Don't you?"

"Maybe someday," I admitted. "But right now I'd rather find Papa."

"What for?"

"Well, for one thing because I'm worried about him. I haven't seen him for over seven months and something could have happened to him. For another thing, now that I'm nineteen, I'm too old to continue living with Mrs. Worthing.

"Is she making you leave?" Janey asked, her eyes widening in amazement."

"Don't be a goose, of course not. But I don't like being dependent on her hospitality."

"Would you travel with your Papa?"

"I think so, if he'd let me. I'm able to take care of myself now so I wouldn't be any trouble to him."

Janey started to argue that point when Mrs. Worthing stuck her head back inside the door.

"Victoria, run down to the stables and tell the boys it's time to eat."

Thankful for a chance to escape outside for a few minutes, I untied my apron and flung it onto a stool. Stepping out into the warm sunshine, I walked down the path to the stables, past budding trees and new green blades of grass.

I reached the stables and pushed the feedway door open. As I entered the straw-strewn interior, I saw one of the stableboys gathering up small kittens and putting them into a gunnysack.

"What are you doing?" I asked curiously.

"Got to drown 'em," he replied before turning his head slightly to spit out tobacco.

I digested this information as he put the rest of the litter into the sack. "Please don't do that," I wheedled.

He straightened and knotted the sack. "Got to," he declared before spitting again.

"No," I cried, surprising him with an unexpected lunge for the sack.

He drew back hastily and held it over his head, well out of my reach. "We got two good mousers now and that's all we need. If these 'uns live, they'll jest go wild and 'ungry," he explained testily.

Unswayed by his logic, I made another grab for the sack and overbalanced him. We toppled into a rolling heap in the straw, each of us intent on gaining control of the lost sack.

"What's the trouble here?" a voice broke in sharply.

29

I looked up to see Lord Linton leading his horse into a stall and throwing the reins to a groom. "He's going to drown those poor kittens." I motioned helplessly to the sack as the stableboy regained control of it.

"There's too many cats now, your lordship," the stableboy explained, rising with a fawning smile that revealed brown tobacco stains on his teeth.

"Milord, please stop him," I pleaded.

The marquis glanced disinterestedly from me to the sack. "My, my, it seems to be a case of nobility versus practicality. I myself have always been a practical man." Lord Linton turned abruptly to the stableboy. "Drown them," he pronounced curtly and walked out the door, leaving me staring after him in disbelief.

The boy brushed straw off of his fustian clothes before favoring me with a triumphant look. I rose slowly and started out the door, taking the path to the cottage. Tears pricked at my eyelids. "It's so cruel," I whimpered aloud. I reached the cottage and paused to stubbornly wipe a tear away before entering. As I stepped inside, my chin began to tremble and I sank blindly down on a cane-bottomed chair and cried in earnest.

A knock on the door startled me. I looked up as the door opened to see the marquis step in. He was carrying a gunnysack which he placed on the stone floor and opened. The furry contents tumbled out, and tiny kittens began to crawl blindly in all directions.

"Oh," I cried. I dried my eyes quickly and dropped to the floor, scooping the kittens into my lap.

"That was all I could manage this trip. The mother

cat will be delivered by coach." He added dryly, "She took strong exception to riding my horse."

"Thank you," I murmured, holding a fuzzy kitten against my cheek. "It was very kind of you."

"Not at all," he replied smoothly, watching me speculatively. "It just came to me that it would be so much nicer to have you thank me than that red-faced stableboy." He lowered his elegant body to the floor beside me and I glanced at him suspiciously. One by one, he removed the kittens from my lap and set them on the floor. Then he pulled me to him. "We're alone now," he said pleasantly as he bent and kissed me.

It was a short, sweet kiss which I frankly enjoyed. I pursed my lips to receive another one. He was about to oblige when the sound of wheels outside caused him to jump up, pulling me with him. In a moment a knock sounded and the defeated stableboy entered carrying a hissing cat by the nape of the neck at arm's length. He dropped the cat and she retreated in fury to the far side of the room. After a moment of glaring at us, she started to circle the room, cautiously exploring. Finding the kittens, she began to bathe them with her tongue, making guttural purring noises in her throat.

"The housekeeper says you're to return to the house at once," the stableboy announced in a nasty voice.

"Was that order directed to myself?" Lord Linton asked coldly.

"Oh, n-no, not you, s-sir—the girl," he stammered in confusion.

"I shall return anyway and you may take this young lady back with you in the coach." He turned and was gone.

I followed the scowling lad out to the coach. Even in my confused state, I appreciated the lovely blue velvet of the squabs and giggled to myself at the thought of the stir which I would cause by arriving in such style back at the manor house.

I did create a stir back at the house, but it was not at all the proper kind of attention. Mrs. Worthing asked some very direct questions about what I was doing riding about the countryside in the marquis's carriage when I was supposed to be hard at work at the house. After she left, Janey made some impertinent suggestions about what his lordship and I might have been doing at the cottage. I had confided the escapade to Janey, although I had told Mrs. Worthing nothing about being alone with Lord Linton at the cottage.

"Do you expect me to believe that he made a special trip to your cottage just to bring you a few kittens and he had nothing else on his mind?" Janey interrogated for the third time.

"I don't know what he had on his mind, Janey. I've told you he simply felt bad about having the kittens drowned and he brought them to me to keep."

"Sure, sure. Let's go back to the part where you were rolling around on the floor."

"We were not rolling around on the floor!" I denied vehemently.

"You said you kissed him," she accused.

"I did."

"On the floor," she pursued.

"Yes, we just happened to be on the floor. But you make it sound so—" I broke off at a loss for the right word. "Well, you have simply mistaken the matter."

"Give over, Victoria. The man's a rake and quite a

handsome one at that. And you're an innocent he means to attempt."

"I can handle myself, thank you," I sniffed.

"I doubt it," she flung over her shoulder as she left the elegant drawing room.

I resumed dusting. Janey was right. I should not have allowed the marquis to kiss me, or worse yet, returned his kiss so warmly. A girl who would allow a man in her house when no one else was about and then dally with him on the floor must be considered fast in any circle. What must he think of me now! He had been kind to bring me the kittens—a gift which Mrs. Worthing had not regarded as altogether a blessing—but he was not the type of person to give something for nothing. A little voice warned me that kindnesses from him could prove to be very dangerous items of barter.

"Victoria, can you go to the village for a few items?" Mrs. Worthing asked me as she took the dusting rag out of my hands and replaced it with a list. I had been leaning with my elbows on a mahogany tilt-top table, staring out the window, my dusting wholly forgotten.

"Yes, of course I'll go. Should I finish dusting first?"

"No, I need the items today," she returned tartly.

I removed my crumpled apron and straightened my brown cotton dress. "I'll be back before you know it," I predicted cheerfully.

"We'll see," she answered skeptically.

I went out the heavy oak front door, waving to the footman and a cooing Virginia, and bounded down the wide gray steps, stalking across the vast expanse of green lawn on a shortcut through the woods to the village.

Chilhan was a pleasant town with gracious timbered houses surrounding the square at the top of the village. It boasted an old inn as well as a four-hundred-year-old church. Nestled among beech trees were the keep of a Norman castle and the largest and oldest heronry in England.

I had reached the village and started into the shop when I was stopped by someone calling my name. I turned to see Mrs. Hanthorne, the vicar's wife, approaching me with steady if weighty gait. As she reached me, she paused to pant for several seconds, resting her bulky frame against the side of the building. "Goodness, I'm completely out of breath."

I waited patiently as she continued panting.

"Well now," she managed to say, "how are you?"

"I'm fine." I smiled uncertainly.

"Good, good. And how is life in the elegant home of Lord Linton?"

"Fine." I hoped our conversation would be of short duration since she always made me feel vaguely uncomfortable.

"I should like to hear all the details of what it's like to live in the same house with such a god."

"I don't live at the manor house, Mrs. Hanthorne. I live at the cottage with Mrs. Worthing."

She swept a hand impatiently across her face. "With him, near him, what is the difference?" I was about to explain when she continued, "What I want to know is, what is he like? My dear Angelique would make a lovely machioness, and I'm most anxious for Lord Linton to meet her. When do you think that would be possible?" She regarded me hopefully.

"I haven't any idea," I answered blankly.

She took another deep breath of air and began again. "I particularly wish Lord Linton to meet Angelique. I don't know whether you are aware of the fact, but her grandfather was a baronet. Since that makes her quality, I'm certain that Lord Linton would like to meet her above all things."

"I'm certain that he would," I agreed, feeling far from certain that this was true but also feeling quite trapped.

"Then when do you think I should bring her up to Meadowacres? I had thought to wait for the marquis to call on us himself, but so far he hasn't, which I must say I think is the outside of enough. The man has been here three weeks and the very least he could do is come round to meet the vicar."

At a loss for words I merely nodded.

"So do you think tomorrow is a good time?"

"A very good time, no doubt, but you see, Mrs. Hanthorne, I'm really not in a position to—"

"Tomorrow it is then. Good day, Victoria."

She turned abruptly, the plume of her large purple hat brushing across my nose as she did, and proceeded back down the street from whence she had come. I looked after her helplessly. Angelique Hanthorne, a shy girl whose only resemblance to her mother was in size, was not the sort of person I thought my employer would be anxious to meet. The girl was six and twenty and had been on the shelf for a good three years in spite of her mother's best efforts. I sighed and proceeded on into the store, hoping that Mrs. Hanthorne would not mention my name in connection with her visit.

35

My purchases made, I started back to the estate. For a week now I had successfully avoided Lord Linton. If I heard his voice down the vast hall, I beat a hasty retreat. The result was that I had not seen him since our meeing at Mrs. Worthing's cottage. Not that there was probably any need to continue such measures. No doubt he had already completely forgotten about me, but the thought of him made me uneasy, and I wanted to escape any further confrontation with him.

The marquis wasn't my only problem now. I had another one in the form of a large, dull-witted gardener's helper who had fallen top over tail in love with me. His sudden devotion made me the butt of Janey's jokes and made walks in the garden hazardous expeditions. I kept a wary eye out for him as I neared the manor house.

I reached the back of the house and safely proceeded into the hallway, winding my way over to the kitchen. "I've brought the things you needed," I announced as I entered.

"Took you long enough," Mrs. Worthing noted, looking up from a fowl she was basting.

"It wasn't my fault. I ran into Mrs. Hanthorne and she wanted to know about Lord Linton."

"Dear Lord, no. I hope you told her his lordship had removed back to London for the duration."

"Not exactly," I admitted as I sampled a freshly made cookie. "She's coming to call tomorrow."

Mrs. Worthing shook her head. "She has mistaken the matter if she thinks the master is going to display any interest in poor Angelique," she observed crisply.

"Perhaps she won't come after all," I suggested hopefully.

"No doubt," Mrs. Worthing rejoined, "and perhaps the Prince Regent will drop by the cottage tomorrow for tea."

CHAPTER FOUR

The next morning proved my optimistic wish mistaken. Mrs. Hanthorne appeared at the front door wearing an outrageous red dress with tiny puff sleeves and a dangerously scooped neckline. In tow was Angelique looking disastrous in a white dress with dozens of flounces and a square neck decorated with rosy pink ribbons that made her pasty complexion look even more sallow. Janey saw their carriage arriving through the drawing room window and summoned me to witness the spectacle. We could hear the dignified butler inquire their names as Mrs. Hanthorne haughtily told him that they had come to visit his lordship. They were led off down the hall.

"Whatever do you think of that?" Janey asked.

"I think someone should have warned his lordship they were coming."

"I daresay surprise attacks are the only advantage they have now that Angelique is an ape leader," Janey observed.

Mrs. Worthing's approaching footsteps sent us both scurrying.

I hastened down to the library to continue the cleaning that the Hanthornes' arrival had interrupted.

Humming to myself, I resumed dusting one by one the brown leather wing chairs grouped about the tiled fireplace, taking great care with the massive wooden legs that were carved at the bottom to resemble a lion's claw. I had just finished the last one when the door opened and Lord Linton marched in. His face had a distinctly menacing look on it as he turned his gaze on me before slamming the door and leaning against it.

I rose hastily from the floor and looked about wildly for a retreat.

"What did you mean inviting that woman here?" he barked.

"I didn't!" I sputtered. "Do you think I invited her here?"

"How quickly you grasp things," he sneered. "She told me she was expressly invited by a member of my household and when I inquired whom, she gave your name. Do you deny it? You are Victoria, are you not?" His tone was positively ferocious.

I took a step backward. "Yes! No! That is, I do deny it, but I am Victoria."

He stalked over to one of the Chippendale chairs and leaned on the back of it, looking evenly into my scared face. "I take leave to tell you that I do not appreciate people meddling in my affairs."

"I didn't," I denied, shaking my head so fiercely my hair fell out of its ribbon and hung about my shoulders.

He turned and paced the floor for several minutes. In the lengthening silence I shifted my weight uncomfortably from foot to foot. Timidly I offered, "I'm sorry that she came to call on you, but surely there are worse things?"

"I'm coming to them," he informed me coldly. "Not only did she come to my house without my invitation, but she brought along her poor chit of a daughter and proceeded to embarrass us both by talking at some length about grandfathers and baronets and Quality marrying Quality." He ceased pacing and glared at me.

Anxious to redeem myself, I began to clarify Mrs. Hanthorne's remarks. "You see, sir, her grandfather was a baronet and—"

He cut me off with an angry, dismissive gesture. "Have you anything to say for yourself?" he snapped.

"I didn't invite them." I made a weak protest. "I saw her on the street, and she stopped me and said she was coming."

He searched my face briefly. The biting harshness died in his own face as I watched in trepidation. In a completely rational voice he said, "No. Of course you didn't invite her. An overbearing she-wolf like that would hardly need an invitation." He regarded the Aubusson carpet for a moment and then surprised me with a short laugh. "So, after all these days of avoiding me, you are finally trapped in a room with me."

"How did you know I was avoiding you?" I asked, surprise overcoming discretion.

"Ah, you confess," he said sardonically. "Well, truth to tell, I didn't notice for a day or so. Then I began to realize that there was often a bustle of skirts just before I entered a vacant room to find the opposite door ajar. Or, I would enter the front hall in time to see the heel of a dainty foot hastening around the back corner. I thought something was a little smoky and then I realized that I had not seen you about the house since the arrival of this mysterious person."

I stared uncertainly at the floor. He didn't sound angry but perhaps he was. I stood waiting for a reprimand that never came. Instead he said, "If you don't mind, perhaps you could clean somewhere else. Just now I need to use the library."

Puzzled, I nevertheless made the most of my opportunity, throwing him a grateful glance as I rushed from the room. I could hear his laughter as I closed the door.

That was my last bit of excitement for a whole week. I must admit that I found the novelty of calmness quite relaxing. But my respite was broken when I found myself embraced in the small grove of dogwood trees outside the garden.

"Jake, please," I murmured as I attempted to extract my hand from the bearlike paw that encased it.

"You're so pretty, Victoria. Just let me hold your hand for a minute."

Jake had tracked me to the grove of dogwoods from his post in the garden and was attempting to declare his undying love as I squirmed uncomfortably.

"What's the matter?" he asked, hurt. "Don't you like me?"

"I looked up into his rather vacant brown eyes set in a large, cherubic face. "Of course I like you, Jake, but that's not the same as—"

"Unhand that child," Mrs. Worthing commanded, following up on her order with a brisk whack from her broom across the surprised young man's backside.

"Ouch! There's no call to be violet," he remonstrated.

42

"That's violent," she corrected, "and I shall be more than that if you do not remove yourself this instant."

"But, ma'am," my knightly giant pleaded with the tiny, plump woman before him.

"Get!" my latter-day David ordered.

He trudged off, throwing a baleful look back to me.

"He doesn't mean any harm, Mrs. Worthing," I explained, "but, you see, he's in love with me and he's trying to tell me."

"These foreign boys are turning the place upside down. What with gardeners and footmen and stable-hands from all counties it's a wonder we go on as well as we do. Chilham boys are bad enough, but at least we know their families," she huffed as she led the way back to the house. "I can't be everywhere at once—with Virginia smitten by that gangling footman and you in the copse with that big idiot and Lord knows where Janey is . . ." She paused for breath as we reached the back of the house. Leading the way in, she resumed, "You'll have to polish the silver. The guests will be arriving at any minute."

"Please, Mrs. Worthing," I protested, "I polished all day yesterday. I have blisters that have blisters—whole families of blisters—and I may never be able to use my hands again." I ended on a pathetic note.

Unmoved, Mrs. Worthing handed me a polishing cloth and pointed toward the dining room. I started reluctantly down the long portrait-lined hall.

"Victoria," she called after me, "I believe you'll find you can watch the guests arriving from the dining room and if I'm not mistaken I hear carriage wheels now."

I turned back to see her blue eyes twinkling in a

smile. I answered with a smile before hurrying on to the dining room in time to rush to the window and see a vehicle pulling up in front of the house. A man swung down from his high perch and pulled off his beaver hat, revealing curly reddish hair. I recognized him as the young man I had overheard with Lord Linton in the garden. He tossed his hat boyishly to Lord Linton as the marquis descended the steps and came forward to clap a hand on his friend's shoulder.

I pulled the window open and leaned forward past the lovely green drapes to watch in fascination.

"I might have known you'd drive a phaeton down instead of coming sedately in a carriage," the marquis said good-naturedly.

They mounted the steps into the house and, as the door closed behind them, I saw another conveyance coming down the tree-lined drive. A short time later an elegant carriage with an elaborate crest on the side pulled into the drive. An older couple alighted and then a brown-haired girl about my age. The woman was large, both tall and heavy, and dressed in a canary-yellow dress that matched her suspiciously bright yellow hair. The brown-haired girl was wearing a pale blue dress which emphasized her boyishly slim figure. The man stood uncertainly by the side of the carriage, clasping his hat.

"Belinda," the woman called loudly, "do find my vinaigrette. I feel quite faint from such a long ride."

Belinda searched dutifully in a reticule as her mother waited impatiently. Producing the vinaigrette, she held it out, announcing, "Here it is, Mama."

At that precise moment Lord Linton appeared and

44

approached the threesome. "I trust the trip has not been too great a strain, Lady Markby?" he asked pleasantly.

"No, it was quite lovely," she answered in equally pleasant tones before turning to her daughter and saying in a less dulcet voice, "Put that thing away, Belinda. I don't need a restorative." She turned back to the marquis, resuming her smile. "I have a strong constitution, of course, and Belinda does too for all her delicate looks. Would you believe she's the picture of health and never sick."

"I'm certain she is," he answered amiably.

"She'll make some lucky man an excellent wife," Lady Markby continued.

"Mama, please," the girl pleaded.

"I've no doubt she will," Lord Linton agreed as he offered his arm to Lady Markby. The father and daughter trailed up the steps behind them.

I had scant time to wonder just how Belinda might fit into the marquis's life because four more carriages arrived in rapid succession. First an elderly man, then a family with three young children, and then two more young gentlemen. Altogether I thought it an odd assortment. I had expected Lord Linton's friends to be younger and perhaps wilder looking than the staid group of people who had arrived. Of course, the young men might yet prove to be exceptionable, but at first glance they seemed to be all that was proper, impeccably dressed and very dignified.

My thoughts were interrupted as Janey breezed into the room. "Did you see them?"she asked excitedly.

"Yes."

"I see there's at least one matchmaking Mama. She'll have his lordship leg-shackled to that pug-nosed daughter if she has her way."

"Was she pug-nosed? I couldn't tell from here."

Janey looked at me with a suppressed smile. "Now what difference would it be making to you what she looks like? You're not becoming sweet on the master, are you?"

"No, of course not," I laughed. "With my position and my background he'd never pay the slightest heed to me."

She shrugged. "I've heard there are women in London who didn't have a feather to fly with until they made the proper match. And you're certainly pretty enough to attract a man's attention. And I'll bet you're every bit as well educated as that Markby chit—so she doesn't need to go getting uppity," Janey ended defiantly as she turned and swept from the room.

I smiled. Poor Belinda wasn't faring at all well, I decided. Not only was she pushed around by her mama but now she was accused of being uppity by someone she had never met.

As I turned back to my task of polishing, I considered what Janey had said about my education being equal to Belinda's. One of Papa's traveling companions after Mama died had been a gently bred but bawdy-natured lady named Lucy. She had been presented at court during her first Season in London, and for the first month or so had attempted to behave like a proper society lady. But it wasn't in her nature to be docile or missish, and she soon attached herself to a set of wild young men. She attended cockfights dressed as

46

a boy and even went to the Westminister rat pit to watch the famous dog Billy kill the rats. In a very short time her exploits became so well known that she was not received in polite society. Undaunted by that fact, she abandoned society altogether and took to traveling about gypsy-fashion. During the three years she was with us, she taught me how to read and write, and when she finished with that, she began to teach me genteel manners and a very upper-class diction.

A blister popped as I rubbed vigorously on a silver ladle. I put the injured finger in my mouth, sucking it gently. "That's it," I announced to the assembled silverware. "All of you go back where you came from." I began to put the pieces in the small, square mahogany chest.

Janey stuck her head inside the door. "Stop ordering the silverware about and come along out of there. The guests will be down before long and Mrs. Worthing wants to set the table herself this first evening."

I obeyed, trailing down the hall after Janey's bobbing red head.

"I heard you were in the garden with Jake," she said. "If I were you, I'd set my sights a little higher. Have you thought about the head gardener? I know he's a little older, but he would be able to support you in better style."

"A little older?" I asked incredulously. "The man's fifty."

"He's not a day over forty-five," Janey argued as I followed her out the back door.

"Where are we going?" I asked.

"Home for the day."

"So soon?"

47

"Yes, Mrs. Worthing said to leave. She thinks if we stay, we'll end up doing something foolish like hiding behind the curtains in the dining room to be present for dinner."

"Oh."

Janey started across the lawn toward the village. "One last thing," she called.

"Yes?"

"Jake's waiting for you on the lane to the cottage so you had better go the long way around."

"Thanks, Janey." Since the possibility of being set upon by footpads seemed more acceptable than another encounter with Jake, I followed Janey's advice and made a wide circle through the forest and crept stealthily in the back door of the cottage.

CHAPTER FIVE

"That woman thrusts her daughter shamelessly at his lordship," Virginia gossiped as we both loitered in the foyer.

"What does he do?" I asked curiously.

"Oh, as to him, he treats her kindly but with no marked interest." She dropped her voice to a throaty whisper. "He has a woman in London who is more to his taste."

"How do you know that?" I demanded.

"Luther told me. Besides, Belinda Markby is eighteen and the master is at least thirty. He don't want no green girl for a wife."

"I doubt if he wants a wife at all," I said, remembering Lord Linton's comments about the holy institution of marriage from the talk I had overheard in the garden.

"Mayhap he don't," she shrugged. "Then there's Lord Lynley—the red-haired one. Lady Markby's been eyeing him like she might try for him if it don't work out with his lordship."

"He is handsome, isn't he?" I asked dreamily.

"Not like the master or Luther, but he does all right," she returned in less than enraptured accents.

"I think he's handsome with his red-gold hair, blue eyes, and straight nose. And he has such an honest, happy mouth. He's the perfect size too," I extolled.

"Too short."

"He's the same height as your Luther," I retaliated, using her beloved footman as an example.

The front door opened, and we scurried in two directions as Lord Linton entered. I proceeded to the garden to pick flowers for the table. Five minutes later I was picking steadily and hoping Jake wouldn't find me when I heard the crunch of gravel on the walk. I looked up to see Lord Lynley ambling down the path toward me. I straightened, smiling broadly at him. He halted on the path, looking completely taken aback. After surveying me a moment, he apparently decided I was harmless and continued slowly toward me.

"Lovely morning, isn't it?" I volunteered cheerily.

"Yes, it is. What sort of flowers are those?" he asked, stopping beside me.

I looked up into his pleasant face and tried to steady the quickening of my pulse. "I don't know, but aren't they pretty?" See how blue they are?" I held them out for him to inspect.

"Yes," he said softly. "Just the color of your eyes."

I blushed and dropped part of the bouquet in my confusion. I bent to retrieve them just as Lord Lynley dropped to his knees and began gathering them up.

"Oh, don't get your clothes dirty," I protested, aghast at the thought of him helping me in such demeaning work. "I'll get them."

"A gentleman should never allow a lady to do such a thing."

"I'm not a lady," I corrected swiftly, raising my eyes to look into his.

"I beg to contradict you—although a gentleman never contradicts a lady—dear me, you are putting me in a bind." He smiled so charmingly I nearly dropped the flowers again. "Allow me to introduce myself. I am Edward Lynley."

Dumbly I repeated, "You're Edward Lynley."

"Yes, that's why I took the liberty of introducing myself as such." His voice was full of amusement.

We were still kneeling on the pathway, and suddenly I felt very shy and foolish. There he was in his blue superfine coat, white cravat, and expertly tailored trousers; and here I was in my gray cotton dress with the frayed cuffs and discolored collar. I stood up hastily. "Excuse me, but I must return to the house." I didn't look back as I hurried away, but I could feel his eyes following me. No doubt he thought me the most ridiculous thing he had met in a long time.

I rushed in the back door.

"Where are you going in such a hurry?" Janey asked, blocking my path.

"I've got to put these flowers in a vase," I gasped.

"They won't wilt in the space of five minutes." She looked at my flushed face closely.

"You been in the garden with Jake?"

"No," I denied emphatically.

"Who have you been in the garden with?"

"I just happened to run into Lord Lynley while I was picking flowers."

"Oh you did, did you?" she asked with a definite smirk on her small face.

51

"Yes, I did. Now if you don't mind, I don't have time to talk." I brushed past her and moved on down the hall.

She followed. "Well, tell me what happened. I think he's the most wonderful gentleman I've ever met, not that I've met many. Do you not find him very polite and charming?"

"As a servant in this household I don't think it makes the slightest difference how I find him," I answered in a voice I was trying to make very casual. I reached the front foyer and began to insert flowers into a blue Wedgwood vase.

"You've set your cap for him," she accused.

"Janey, don't be such a goose. I haven't a romantic thought in my head about the man."

"Oh." Janey sounded deflated as she left.

It was a lie. I had noticed Lord Lynley from afar since the moment he arrived to visit the marquis. But that night and in the succeeding nights following my encounter with him in the garden, I began to think of him more and more, dreaming of him falling madly in love with me. In my dreams he made long, impassioned speeches to me, misquoting liberally from poetry and looking soulfully at me with limpid blue eyes. In the daytime I mentally reviewed the dreams, adding and embellishing certain acts and speeches. I even fantasized him proposing and mapped out a splendid wedding. I was planning my imaginary trousseau when my romantic bubble was suddenly burst.

Ten days after I talked with Lord Lynley in the garden, I happened to overhear him speaking with Lord Linton in the library. The door was open when I walked past, and I shamelessly paused to hear what they were saying, picking up a brass bowl on a table outside the door to polish it idly.

"Yes, she is quite tempting, isn't she?" Lord Linton's voice floated out to me.

"At first I couldn't believe she was a servant. Such a beautiful face and exquisite figure! Naturally I assumed she was someone you had picked up for your amusement," Lord Lynley said.

"Don't think I wouldn't like to. However, she lives on the estate with the old housekeeper so it would be rather awkward. Also she's very naïve."

"Yes. I can see that the first problem would be awkward. However, the naïveté is something you could remedy," Lord Lynley replied. I could hear the laughter in his voice.

"I could at that," Lord Linton returned in a lazy drawl.

"And perhaps I could borrow her from time to time," Lord Lynley suggested in a sensual voice.

I very nearly dropped the brass bowl. I might be naïve, but I was not so naïve that I didn't realize they were discussing me in less than flattering terms. I felt like a prize Hereford up for auction.

With nerveless fingers I placed the bowl back down on the lowboy and slipped quietly out the back door. I walked slowly down the lane toward the cottage, experiencing a sick feeling in the pit of my stomach. All of the time I had been idolizing Lord Lynley he had been thinking of me as an "amusement." He was no different than Lord Linton—both of them wanting to take advantage of an unprotected girl. Their words made me feel common. Mixed with my hurt was a gnawing sense of unease. I knew that as long as I lived on the marquis's estate, I was at his mercy and I didn't want to be at the mercy of a shameless rake.

I reached the cottage and entered wearily. There was no one who could rescue me from this coil. Mrs. Worthing was an employee of Lord Linton's, and I didn't want her to risk his displeasure on my behalf. The other people I knew were also servants with their positions to consider. "Papa," I said aloud as I sank down on my narrow bed. I pondered a moment. Papa could take me away from Meadowacres forever if only he would come back. But he might not be back for some time, I thought in dejection. And in the meantime all I could do was wait like a lamb lost in the woods for Lord Linton, Lord Lynley, or some other of his lordship's libertine friends to take advantage of my vulnerability.

Well, I would not give them the chance. I would leave. I would go to . . . Where would I go? I would just have to find Papa, that was all. I stood up resolved. Yes, I would find Papa. Heartened by my decision, I began to hastily fling clothes into my pillowcase. That finished, I scratched out a note to Mrs. Worthing, took my meager savings from under the dresser scarf, and headed for the coach stop.

Tossing the pillowcase over my shoulder, I walked down the lane to the town, lost in thought. I knew that all of the stages stopped at the Cranberry Inn. My problem was which one to take. Papa had always been partial to the North Country—he could even be in Scotland—but if I went to Scotland, I reasoned, and he wasn't there, then I wouldn't have enough money left to travel back south. I abandoned trying to use logic about Papa's erratic wanderings and decided to embark on the first stage that came through and go in any direction.

I reached the Cranberry Inn just in time to catch a coach. I swung up into it and settled myself in as the horses took off down the road. After putting my pillowcase carefully on the seat beside me, I looked up to find myself being watched curiously by my two fellow passengers. One was a young girl who was fashionably dressed—at least she was dressed in clothes similar to Belinda's and that was the extent of my knowledge of fashion—in a blue gown decorated with white satin ribbons about the scooped neck and flounced hem. Her companion was an older woman—tall, thin, and stern looking—dressed in a drab brown dress.

"Hello," the girl greeted me cheerfully.

"Hello."

"Are you from Chilham?" she demanded but didn't give me time to reply before continuing. "Such a charming village with its timbered houses and quaint lime trees surrounding the churchyard. I've been visiting here," she informed me. "Well, not actually in the village," she corrected conscientiously. "I've been visiting at the manor house of Meadowacres."

I tried to appear nonchalant as I digested this last bit of information. I had not seen this girl at Meadowacres, but I certainly didn't want her to know I was running away from there. "Were you there long?" I ventured cautiously.

"No, I only arrived last night. I had come on a surprise visit to my brother who's staying with a friend, but he packed me back off to London this morning," she complained. "He said it was unthinkable to visit someone without an invitation. He's so stuffy!" She paused indignantly to consider the injustice of her brother's actions. Then, in a more conversational tone, she continued, "He can be a top-of-the-trees fellow when he wants to be. He just objected to my arriving unannounced. What's your name?"

Startled by her abrupt change of subject, I answered hesitantly, "Victoria."

"I'm Maryanne and this is my maid, Ellen Marsh." She nodded toward the older woman. Ellen was regarding me with stiff disapproval. "Where are you going?" Maryanne asked.

Before I had time to speak, her maid interrupted reproachfully, "I'm sure this young lady does not care to discuss her destination with us." Ellen's voice caught briefly on the word "lady" and her perusal of my shabby attire, complete with pillowcase, did little to alter her opinion of my status. I shrank back against the squabs.

Maryanne made no attempt to gloss over Ellen's inference about my social standing. "Well, of course she's not dressed like a lady, but she doesn't have a coarse tongue or crude manners. She speaks as if she's quite well-bred. And don't you think she has the biggest blue eyes, Ellen, and such jet-black hair." Maryanne reached out and touched a lock of my hair, then settled back in her seat. Ellen, who appeared unshaken by the color of my eyes, turned to stare out the window.

Maryânne paid no further heed to her. "I'm returning to London," she informed me, her brown eyes sparkling as she pushed back a lock of red-blond hair struggling to escape from her cheery blue bonnet.

"Indeed," I murmured politely.

"Yes, and it shouldn't be dreary for much longer because the Season will soon be in full swing."

"How nice."

"I'm seventeen," she stated proudly, "and I'll be eighteen this summer, so I'll soon be married and have an establishment of my own."

"You are engaged then?" I asked.

"Not precisely. Actually no, but I shall be presented this Season, and I'm certain I shall take and have any number of offers. It will simply be a matter of choosing which husband I want. Of course, I shall be quite selective as I don't want anyone who is a Tulip of the Town—I couldn't abide a dandy. I only require that my husband be handsome, elegant, rich, even tempered, and head over heels in love with me."

"My late brother-in-law was even tempered," Ellen said in quelling tones. "He was raving mad all of the time."

Maryanne ignored Ellen's barb. "He must also be someone who is a bruising rider and a crack whip and—" She stopped in mid-sentence. "Dear me, I've been rambling on and haven't given you a moment to talk about yourself. Are you going to visit friends?"

"Uh, well, you see I'm not certain," I returned evasively.

"You don't know who you're going to visit?" Her brow furrowed in puzzlement.

"No, I'm on my way to take up a position in a household of some friends of my aunt and uncle," I improvised.

"How interesting. Do tell me more."

"Well they—the people I'm going to work for—have a huge house, nearly twice the size of the manor

57

house at Meadowacres, and a great many servants," I embellished my lie.

"What will your position be?" Maryanne asked.

"My position?" I looked out the window anxiously and providentially spied the slate and thatched roofs of a town looming up ahead. I drew my head back in the window. Fortified by the knowledge that I would shortly be debarking from the carriage, I turned back to Maryanne and said rather haughtily, "I shall be a governess, of course. Naturally I had my choice of several places of employment, but I selected this one because I felt the people were more refined, not so *de trop* as you find in so many households today." I folded my hands primly across my lap in front of me and glanced up to see what effect my little speech had had on Maryanne.

"A governess?" she said respectfully. "That's a very good position, almost a member of the household."

I nodded. I was stopped in the act of bobbing my head up and down by the sardonic expression of disbelief on Ellen's face.

"A governess, you say?" Ellen repeated thoughtfully. "Might I ask the name of your employers?"

"I daresay you wouldn't know them," I stalled as the carriage rolled to a stop and I looked out to see a sign announcing that I had arrived at the Hen and Hawthorne.

"I'm certain I should if they have a house twice as large as Meadowacres. In point of fact, I should say your new employer is at least a royal duke to have such holdings."

The coach door opened. "Oh look," I cried, "there's my aunt and uncle come to meet me. Hello Aunt Lily."

I waved to a couple passing the inn door. "I'm coming," I called after them and bounded down out of the coach.

"I don't think your aunt and uncle saw you," Maryanne said, leaning out the window. "They're rounding the corner."

"I'll catch up with them later. I need to go into the inn just now. So good to have met you. Good-bye now." I waved gaily, then turned and squared my shoulders before marching inside the Hen and Hawthorne to search out the landlord.

CHAPTER SIX

Peeking into a long, dark taproom, I spied a husky man in a dirty white apron sitting alone at a round table. I ventured in cautiously as he took another drink from a tankard in front of him and set it back on the table.

I moved hesitantly up to him. "Sir?"

"What do you want?" he asked in less than sociable tones.

"I'm looking for someone," I began.

He looked bored. "Lots of people come through here." He gestured with his hand around the empty room. "See." He took another drink and gazed thoughtfully at his tankard.

Maryanne's chatter had kept me diverted on the road and I had not had time for a great many doubts. Now, however, fears about the rashness of my actions set in in good earnest.

I took a deep breath and began to describe Papa. "The man I'm looking for is tall, thin, in his late forties. He has very blue eyes and brown hair." I paused to think. "Oh, and he has a tooth missing in front. It was knocked out when he threw himself in front of a horse to rescue a child. He also has a scar on his forehead. He got it when he was trying to save an elderly man from footpads. And he has a limp."

"Which I'm sure he received in honorable combat for his country," the landlord finished dryly.

"No, he—" I began.

"Never mind," he interrupted. "There is a man who somewhat matches that description that's been helping out down at the stables the last few nights."

My eyes widened excitedly. I was almost unable to believe my good luck. "Where are the stables?" I demanded.

He jerked his head disinterestedly in the general direction of the stables, and I took off in a run, bursting through the stable door, shouting, "Papa!"

Silence. As my eyes accustomed themselves to the dim light, I could discern a figure sleeping in a pile of straw in a corner. I hurried over and shook him. "Papa, wake up! It's me, Vicky Ann," I shouted. He turned over slowly and opened his eyes. My heart plummeted. "Oh, it's you, Job," I said forlornly. I had never felt so dejected and completely alone.

He blinked and then blinked again. "And I'm sure I'm mighty glad to see you too," he grumbled. "Come abustin' in here wakin' me up and then sore cause I'm not your papa." He studied me resentfully. "Who are you, anyway?"

"I'm Victoria Lyons, Robert Lyons's daughter, don't you remember?"

He sat up slowly and rubbed his head. "Yeah, I kinda do. Seems to me like you used to go with your pa when he was apreachin' some." He paused reflectively, then continued. "Not much work for preachers these days. Take myself, a man of the cloth, yet here I am aworkin' at a stable instead of spreadin' the word of God." His voice rose oratorically. "But I tell you, the Lord's acomin' back and—"

With an impatience born from a great many long-winded sermons, I interrupted, "Yes, Job, but Papa, have you seen him lately? Do you have any idea where he might be?"

"Eh? Robert Lyons, you say?" He thought a moment. "I haven't seen him since the time we delivered the word of the Lord together at a gathering for lost souls down near Eastbourne."

"How long ago was that?" My spirits rose slightly.

"Well, I don't rightly recall." He scratched his head and straw fell out. "Seems like it was before I fell in with the band of gypsies. Yes, I recollect, it was last November."

"Five months ago?" I asked, dismayed. "Oh, Job, I've got to find Papa. I've nowhere to go." My throat was beginning to constrict and tears were prickling my eyelids.

"Well, don't fret, er, uh, Vivianne. There's goin' to be a gatherin' of the faithful out by them rocks on Salisbury Plains. I'm agoin' and your pa might be there too. You can go with me, and if we cain't find him, might be we'll find someone who knows where he is."

"Oh, thank you, Job!" I smiled, dabbing my eyes. "It's Victoria," I added, just to keep things straight.

"Course ye'll have to travel light," he cautioned.

I thought wryly that he made it sound as if I intended to travel with a full retinue of servants.

"And ye'll have to be ready to leave on short notice. Sometimes people gets suspicious of me, expecially if there's someone around what's amissin' something. People don't understand that the Lord demands part of every man's wages—even if it ain't always freely give."

"I'll do whatever you say. I'll leave in the dead of night if necessary."

He looked at me skeptically. "Another thing. It'll go a good deal easier for us if you get yourself up in a different rig."

I looked doubtfully down at my faded green poplin dress. "What's wrong with me?"

"With a face like that, you're goin' to attract jest the wrong kind of attention." He went off mumbling to himself and returned some minutes later with a baggy blouse and large skirt. Seating himself in the straw, he rummaged among his small pile of belongings until he found a needle and thread. Then he made himself comfortable by crossing his legs and proceeded to sew a sloppy pouch into the skirt. Under his direction I helped him stuff it full of feathers from his pillow.

"I'll turn around whilst ye don your new clothes," Job offered gallantly.

I reluctantly traded them for my own now quite attractive poplin dress. The effect of the new clothes was to make me look as if I had a droopy chest and somewhat weak stomach muscles.

"Good," Job declared as he ambled toward a horse's stall. After a good deal of neighing and snorting Job emerged bearing, of all things, the horse's tail.

"What's that for?" I asked apprehensively.

"A wig," he answered simply, seating himself back in the straw and sewing rapidly.

"But I don't want to wear it," I remonstrated.

"Ye got to," he pronounced as he stood up and came toward me. Pinning the wig to my head, he secured it with a scarf tied gypsy-fashion at the back of my neck. "Here, put this on," he directed, producing a small black piece of cloth on a string.

"What is it?"

"An eye patch." He slipped it over my head.

I felt utterly ridiculous.

Job stepped back and regarded me critically. "Won't have no trouble protectin' you," he declared. "No trouble at all. Come along now."

We left in haste before anyone could find the missing clothes, dismembered pillow, and shorn horse. Job and I slipped out of town and headed west, walking along dusty roads past cottages with thatched roofs, under broad shady trees, through small villages with square houses set close to the road, and out onto the dusty roads again. I was becoming numb, and my traitorous feet were blistering. Blessedly night fell and we found a deserted cottage to sleep in.

The second day we continued to trudge westward. I had ceased to notice the scenery around me. All that I was aware of was my aching body as we tromped along. Around six that evening we stopped at an abandoned barn and Job went for food. He returned carrying a ham with a suspicious-looking piece of cut twine attached to it, carrots with dirt still clinging to them, some eggs, and a warm pie. He spread out a large handkerchief and began to lay out the food. I took the carrots down to a nearby stream and washed them. When I returned, Job was praying over the food, loudly thanking Providence for sending it to us. His voice dropped from a pious wail to a normal tone as I seated myself on the floor.

"Pass the carrots, will ye?"

I handed him a dripping carrot, and he began to chew greedily. The carrot was followed by an egg sucked raw out of the shell. "Every once in a while I git one with a baby chick startin' to grow inside," he chuckled. "Ain't you hungry?"

I watched him eat with waning appetite. "No, not very."

"Here, try this," he offered me a piece of ham.

I took it and began to chew disinterestedly. I was surprised to learn that my appetite was not really diminished at all, and I ate with relish.

As darkness fell, we crept into separate piles of straw and fell asleep. My body relaxed gratefully into the musty straw.

Late that night I was shaken awake to hear Job whispering in my ear, "We've got to make a run for it. The law is after us."

I sprang up wide awake, grabbed my pillowcase, and took Job's hand as he led me through the dark barn and out a back door. We whisked outside just as the other door opened. "Even took my wife's pie that was cooling on the windowsill," I heard a voice complaining. "Can't have folks like that loose. You never know what they'll do next."

We didn't stay to hear more. Job headed for the stream. "We'll have to keep awalkin' until daylight so's they don't find us," Job said when we were some distance from the barn.

I followed close behind him. "What was that noise?" I asked in alarm.

"Jest an owl."

"Oh." The darkness, lit only by the moon when we walked through clearings, was eerie. The dark shapes of trees and bushes ahead looked like figures lurking for us. "You afraid, Job?" I asked. My throat had a funny, tight feeling.

"No, they won't catch us now. Don't ye worry."

I think I would have been relieved to be caught by those nice people back at the barn rather than be left out here to the terrors of the night. To calm myself I tried to make conversation with Job.

"Have you ever been out of England, Job? Not counting Scotland."

"Oncet."

"Where?"

"Spain."

"How was Spain when you were there?"

"South of France," he returned shortly.

I gathered that Job didn't want to indulge in any more light chatter, so I counted trees for the rest of the night.

Four more days and many, many miles later we arrived at Stonehenge. The last day of our journey the road became increasingly crowded with people headed in the same direction. Some passed in donkey carts or on horseback, but most, like us, were on foot. There were mothers with dark Celtic eyes carrying small children and men with black hair and beards smiling and speaking to us as we passed. We also passed old men with long white hair and long white beards as well as old women with wild eyes. Occasionally Job met someone he knew and we fell into step beside them for a time. I listened while they talked of places they had preached together or replayed hands from old card games.

Finally we arrived at Stonehenge late in the evening just as the sun was going down. Job found us space on the ground to stretch out and sleep for the night, and I laid down in exhaustion. People must have streamed into the camp all night long. I slept only fitfully and frequently felt a foot brush across me as someone stepped over me, but the bustling of the camp only served to sustain my high spirits. Surely now that I was here, there must be some way of finding Papa. And since I was here with good and Christian people, I knew God must be looking kindly on my endeavor. That knowledge made my sleep blissful if erratic.

I awoke at about five in the morning. The camp was very still, broken only by a baby's occasional cry. Unfolding myself carefully from my space, I gingerly made my way over sleeping bodies until I had cleared myself of them. In the first tinges of dawn I could see the wondrous stones that comprise Stonehenge. I wandered up to the base of one of the huge rocks and touched it reverently. The rocks were enormous gray sandstones. Counting rapidly, I numbered seventeen standing, ten capped by lintels.

"Magnificent, are they not?" a man's voice beside me marveled.

I turned to see a short, square man with graying hair also regarding the stones in fascination. "I wonder who put them here?" I asked in awe.

"Ah, was it not the poet Michael Drayton who wrote:

> Ill did those mighty men to trust thee with
> their story;
> That hast forgot their names who reared thee
> for their glory.

"What does that mean?"

"It means no one knows for certain who erected these monuments to an ancient and powerful god."

"Oh. Well it was an awful lot of work for whoever did it," I replied matter-of-factly.

"Quite so. The construction of this earthly temple lasted four hundred years. These stones are twenty feet long and weigh more than forty tons apiece. Antiquarians theorize as many as fifteen hundred men may have labored for ten years to transport the stones across Wiltshire, a distance of some twenty-four miles. On the other hand, I presume they were not pressed for time."

I took a second, closer look at my companion. He was wearing a smock frock and sandals, so he was not dressed very differently from a great many of the people here. But there was a quality in him that the other people I had met thus far did not possess.

"Ah, you apprehend that I am not altogether like the other members comprising this religious observance?" he asked smugly.

"That's true," I admitted, "but I didn't mean to give any offense."

"My dear woman, to be set apart from this group of cannibals can not fail to flatter. I come here every year for the vernal equinox, that time of year when day equals night and nature adjusts to the coming spring. This year, however, there is to be an added interest to my expedition because this mob has assembled to recreate the pagan rites which took place here many centuries past."

"You are mistaken, sir," I replied, startled by his words. "These people are all Christians and there will be no pagan festivals."

"My dear good woman, you obviously do not see at all clearly what is about to take place. Begging your pardon—I meant to give no offense about your vision, although it is obvious you have some difficulty physically as well as mentally—but there will be a great many pagan festivals. Tonight they intend to offer a pig on that very altar." He pointed to a stone lying not ten feet away.

I straightened my eye patch with dignity. "I don't see why they should do that."

"Nor do I," he agreed readily. "Everyone knows that the Druids, who most probably built this temple, held the wild pig sacred and would never have sacrificed a pig. It would be so much more appropriate to sacrifice a lamb," he pointed out practically.

"You have mistaken the matter, sir," I returned shocked. "There will be no such heathenlike practices performed here. I myself am with a Christian man and I can assure you that his sole purpose for being here is to bring souls to Christ."

"We shall see," he prophesied.

To my astonishment he was very nearly right. Although no animals were offered that night, a great many strange rituals were performed. All day long men stood preaching to the small groups they could gather. Their preaching was frequently punctuated with spectacular cures from miracle waters which they offered to sell for a small price. One girl was able to see after being blind since birth. The cure was so complete that she was able to identify the color blue although she had never seen it before. I vacated that group when someone suggested that I be cured of my bad eye.

As the sun went down that evening, a man in a long white robe talked to his dead mother. I listened in fascination as she instructed him to take up a collection from all present for the salvation of souls in India. Next a man in a black robe emblazoned with gold moons and stars actually ate fire. I was awestruck.

"I've seen that trick before," Job mumbled from his seat on the ground beside me.

"It's not a trick," I denied. "He really ate it."

"You don't eat fire and live," Job pointed out reasonably. "And that man didn't talk to his mother either."

"Of course he did. I heard her speak."

"How come she had such a throaty voice?" he challenged.

"Maybe she had a cold."

"Since when do dead people have colds?" Job demanded. "That man can talk out of both sides of his mouth and sometimes when he's talkin', you can't see his lips move.

"That's impossible," I maintained staunchly.

"Suit yourself," he shrugged, "but don't give these men all your money. No wonder honest Christians like myself can't make a go of it. You got to have a gimmick nowadays," he lamented.

By the third day Job had given up spreading God's

71

word in favor of a lengthly and sometimes loud card game that was continuous from early in the afternoon until late at night. He took breaks from it only long enough for an occasional foray out to the edge of the crowd to watch the never-ending cockfights.

Since that left me to my own devices, I combed the ever-growing crowd, looking for Papa and making inquiries about him. A few people claimed to know him, but no one could give me his direction. By the end of the day my confidence was waning. If I didn't find Papa, I didn't know what I would do. I couldn't stay with Job indefinitely and I couldn't return to Meadowacres. Mrs. Worthing had no doubt told Lord Linton that I was gone, and he probably considered himself well rid of me.

I slept badly that night.

CHAPTER SEVEN

The next morning I began another anxious search for Papa. I was questioning an elderly man when a voice behind me broke in curtly.

"Are you enjoying yourself?"

I reeled to find myself looking into the cold stare of Lord Linton's eyes. I thought he had been angry over Mrs. Hanthorne's visit, but that didn't hold a candle to the way he was looking at me now. I backed away from him a step. The old man I had been addressing looked suspiciously from me to Lord Linton and shuffled away with several backward glances. Lord Linton's gaze never left my face. He reached out and grabbed my arm above the elbow and steered me roughly through the crowd to the outer edges. Still grasping my arm, he jerked me around to face him.

"Why are you here?" I gasped.

His face was harsh as he bit back his answer. "I am here because I returned from my morning ride a sennight ago to find my house in even more of an uproar than I have grown to expect with that menagerie of servants. Mrs. Worthing had returned to her cottage to find some half-cocked note saying you had left. She seemed to think that you would have a hard time

73

fending for yourself, and she all but ordered me to go after you."

"But there was no need to come after me. I explained in my note that I had come to find Papa. When I find him, he'll take care of me." I tried hard to keep the waver out of my voice.

"All that I could gather from your note was that you could no longer work in my household and you were throwing yourself on the mercy of the world."

"I didn't say that!" I protested. "Did Mrs. Worthing tell you that?"

"Not precisely. It was hard to tell exactly what the gist of the letter was, with her waving it in my face and wringing her hands. That was what I could gather, though."

"Oh," I said in a small voice. Then, "How did you find me?"

His tone was dry when he responded. "It wasn't hard. I traced you from the Cranberry Inn to the Hen and Hawthorne. From there it got even more interesting. The landlord at the Hen and Hawthorne was the only person in town who could describe you as a blue-eyed charmer but he did say you asked directions to a certain stablehand. That stablehand had decamped in the company of—from all descriptions—a rather ludicrous-looking person. However, it's an odd stablehand who has perversions which include mutilating a pillow and, shall we say, defacing a horse. I decided there was more to that story than met the eye, begging your pardon. It wasn't hard to follow an old man and a one-eyed hag to Stonehenge. After all, the other misfits were all headed this way."

74

"What are you going to do now?" My voice sounded dreadfully timid to my own ears and had not at all the ring of defiance I wished to convey.

"If I had any sense at all, I would leave you here," he snapped. "However, I am trying to establish myself in the good graces of the townspeople and bringing home the prodigal daughter seems to be a good way to do that."

I looked up at him with tears in my eyes. "But I don't want to go back with you, milord. I want to find Papa."

"Listen, you little numskull. Looking for him in this crowd of pious sinners would be a waste of time. The only biblical phrase any of them ever practiced is 'He was a stranger and I took him in.' I'll take you back to Meadowacres and after the smoke clears here we'll find your father."

"Do you promise?" I asked skeptically.

"Yes," he answered curtly.

"Cross your heart?" I persisted.

"If you don't come with me this instant, I'm going to cross that tender young body of yours with a horse-whip. Do you understand?"

He sounded frighteningly serious so I nodded. "I'll come, but first let me tell Job I'm leaving."

We made our way over to the card game, where Job was seated on the ground with three other players in the midst of a heated discussion over the legality of a card that had just been played.

"I say the queen of hearts has already been played," a large, dark man challenged.

"That was last game," Job reminded him glibly.

"And I say it was this game!"

"Job," I said timidly.

"Jest a minute, Vivianne, I'm busy." He turned back to his fellow card player stormily. "Air ye accusin' me of cheatin'?"

"I am," the man roared.

"Job, please," I tried again.

"Jest a minute, Vera," Job said over his shoulders, then turned his attention back to his detractor. "Well now, I don't take kindly to bein' called a cheater. Matter of fact, I won't play with them what says I cheat."

"I say you cheat," the man countered, leaning forward menacingly, his swarthy face dark with anger.

"In that case I won't play," Job announced and began to scoop coins toward himself.

"Hold one minute there," the dark man screamed. "I say you didn't win that money fair."

"I know what you think," Job answered patiently. "That's why I'm only takin' half the money. You can't say that's not fair, now can ye? I'm agivin' you the benefit of the doubt."

"Job," I repeated.

"Comin'," he assured me as he stood up. "As ye can see, I'm needed, or I should certainly stay and finish this talk," he informed the cardplayers before half sprinting to the site of our meager pile of belongings. Lord Linton and I followed. Job began hastily picking up his things.

"We'd best be packin'. I believe it's time we move along," he said with several glances through the crowd toward the cardplayers.

"Job, that's what I'm trying to tell you. I'm not going with you. I'm going with Lord Linton."

For the first time Job noticed the tall man with dark hair and clothes which were decidedly inappropriate for the occasion, consisting as they did of a fine brown riding outfit and boots that reflected their tiny gold tassels in their shine.

"You say you're goin' with him?"

"Yes."

"Wise choice," he mumbled as he bent to gather the remainder of his possessions.

I picked up my pillowcase and swung it over my shoulder as Lord Linton walked over to Job and said something in low tones.

"Mighty kind of ye," Job replied with a deferential smile.

Lord Linton said something else indistinguishable, and I saw some coins change hands. As we left, Job was smiling more broadly and calling warm thanks after the marquis. I trailed after his lordship, feeling an odd mixture of relief at leaving, dread of the marquis, and an irrelevant curiosity of what Job's chaperonage had cost Lord Linton.

We threaded our way through the crowd to a large stone where a horse was tied. Without a word the marquis grabbed me by the waist and threw me up into the saddle. Then he swung himself up after me and we were off down the road. He muttered something about it being a wonder the horse hadn't been stolen and then lapsed into silence. When we reached the next town, he spoke with the landlord at the inn and led me to the parlor.

Once inside the tiny parlor Lord Linton stalked to the window and stared stonily out of it. I lowered myself quietly into a hard wooden chair and studied the room. It had bare wooden floors with a small hand-braided rug in front of one of the straight chairs. I didn't think it was the type of establishment the marquis usually frequented.

Outside the window I could see darkness closing in. Surely no coach would go tonight, but Lord Linton had said nothing about staying the night at the inn. But then, I thought wryly, he had not discussed most of his plans with me.

"Victoria?" The sound of my name startled me. "Why did you run away?" His voice was matter-of-fact.

"To find my father," I answered honestly.

"You hadn't seen your father for some months. Why did you leave on that particular day?"

"I don't know," I returned weakly.

He stood up abruptly. "I have secured rooms for the night. The landlady will show you to your room and assist you should you require it."

I nodded. The door opened as if in response to a summons and a matronly woman entered.

"Show Miss Lyons to her room," Lord Linton directed.

"Yes, sir," the good woman replied in complete wonder of her distinguished visitor. "Will you be wanting anything special for yourself?"

"No, thank you." He turned back to me. "Miss Lyons, I wish to leave by seven in the morning and I expect you to be ready."

"Yes, milord," I murmured, wondering how I dared be anything but ready after such a command. I trailed after the landlady up the narrow stairs to a small, neat room with white chintz curtains. Pulling off my eye patch and scratching wig, I laid down in my mussed dress and fell asleep before I had time to fully savor the comfort of sleeping in a real bed for a delightful change.

I arose early the next morning, splashed cold water from the pitcher onto my face, dressed in a calico print dress, and combed my hair back from my face. I had long since lost all of my hairpins and was unable to control the small ringlet curls that leaped forward to frame my face in merry abandon at being released from their prison of horsehair. Pushing them back severely a time or two, I finally gave up the effort and trudged downstairs to meet my fate.

My fate was already pacing in the small parlor on the first floor.

"Ah, the inestimable Miss Lyons, and without eye patch, wig, and bulk," Lord Linton greeted me caustically. "May I say I find their absence an improvement in your appearance. Come along now, I don't want to keep the horses waiting. Someone passing might see them and decide to make glue out of them." He took my arm and led me out to a gray carriage. It was obviously hired under duress and compared to his own, it was shabby indeed.

He helped me in and seated himself beside me as the carriage swayed forward. I felt every jolt; it must have been totally without springs, and tufts of horsehair stuck through the worn cushions. I plucked at some of the hair that was scratching my arm.

"I wonder if that's from the same horse you borrowed your hair from?" he asked sardonically.

I looked at him reproachfully.

Surprisingly his cynical mask dropped to reveal a

more human face. "All right, I won't torment you. I collect that you have been through enough at the hands of our card-playing friend and that mob of vagabonds. We shall call a truce until we arrive back at Meadowacres. Then I wish to speak quite directly to you."

I swallowed hard. "Yes, milord."

In anticipation of Lord Linton's proposed talk with me, I worried. He looked out the window as the countryside rolled past, but my spirits were so low I wasn't even interested in the scenery. He had promised he would help me find Papa, but would he? Had he made such a long trip to find me because Mrs. Worthing had asked him to, or because he wanted to punish me for running away? The questions circled in my head like birds of prey circling a helpless victim. I rubbed my eyes and leaned back against the cushions. I heard the soft patter of a drizzling rain as it began to fall on the roof of the carriage. My head nodded.

I awoke later to find my head resting against Lord Linton's shoulder. Straightening hastily, I apologized. "I'm so sorry," I murmured as I nervously brushed his shoulder with quick little flicks of my hand. "I didn't mean to fall asleep on you."

His green eyes glinted in suppressed amusement. "As we were not engaged in any very fascinating conversation, I did not find it at all disturbing that you dozed off. Do you know that you snore?"

I brushed my long hair away from my face and assumed an air of dignity. "I do not think it gentlemanly of you to remark upon events which occur while I am asleep."

He surveyed me with lazy humor. "You may thank your lucky stars that I am a gentleman and that your snoring is the only event which occurred while you were asleep that I have to remark upon."

I turned my shocked face to the window and looked out into the mist.

CHAPTER EIGHT

Two days later I arrived back at Meadowacres. Mrs. Worthing welcomed me back tearfully and bundled me off to the cottage. My relief at escaping Lord Linton was short-lived. He sent instructions that he wished to see me the next morning in the library at the manor house.

"I don't want to go," I whined to Mrs. Worthing as she bustled about the tiny kitchen, fussing over me and wrapping more covers about my already enshrouded figure.

"You could have caught a terrible chill," she chided as she heaped another cover on.

"Mrs. Worthing, I'm suffocating," I protested from under an avalanche of quilts.

"Nonsense. Your little hands feel like ice. Wasn't there even a lap robe in the carriage?"

"I'm afraid it wasn't the height of luxury. There were barely seats in the carriage," I recalled ruefully.

She bristled. "I shall tell his lordship exactly what I think of his carelessness to you."

"No! Don't even mention my name to him. I don't want to be drawn to his attention any more than is absolutely necessary."

"Drawn to his attention!" she sputtered. "As if he's likely to forget you for some time to come. You gave us all a terrible fright, you know. We couldn't imagine what had happened to you. And that ape that works in the garden was inconsolable, blubbering and carrying on something fierce the whole time you were gone."

My mind was still occupied with my biggest problem. "Mrs. Worthing, couldn't you tell Lord Linton that I won't be able to see him for a day or so? I don't feel at all up to going to the great house."

"Indeed I shall," she said with spirit. "I shall also tell him that if he had taken better care of you on the trip back, you wouldn't be in such poor health now. I shall further say that it is my firm belief that you have contacted consumption from your journey."

I resigned myself. "I'll see him tomorrow," I sighed.

The next morning, after a sleepless night, I walked stiffly into the library. The marquis was seated behind a massive walnut desk, his expression stern and his voice unpromising as he began, "Sit down, Miss Lyons. I have something to say to you." He indicated a brown leather chair.

I sat. A great lump was forming in my throat. I could not help but think that anything Lord Linton said to me would end in disaster. Perhaps he even meant to turn me over to the authorities. After all, I had been indirectly involved with Job in theft. Did the marquis know that? I was so lost in my apprehensions that I missed the first few words he spoke. I was pulled back into reality to hear him apologizing to me.

". . . I should never have acted to you the way I

did, and it is up to me to make up to you any personal anguish I may have caused. It is not practical for you to remain employed in this household. Even if I were a veritable saint—which I am not—my friends are not to be entirely trusted with a chit like you around. Do you understand?"

I understood nothing, but I nodded vigorously.

"I have decided to send you to London."

I gasped. "Oh no, please, milord! Give me another chance. I don't know anyone in London. I should starve." The fear in my voice caused Lord Linton to look at me in surprise.

"Do you think I would send you off to London to starve? Good God, what sort of creature have I shown myself to you?" he asked incredulously. More firmly he added, "You are going to stay with some friends of mine."

"Thank you, I shall do very good work. You won't regret this," I assured him in abundant relief.

"Stop acting like a grateful puppy about to lick my hand and listen for a minute," he commanded. "You are to be a guest in their house; you will not be working at all."

"A guest? I don't understand. I don't know them, why should they wish to have me as their guest?"

"Because I have asked them to," he answered testily. As his patience did not seem proof against many more outbreaks from me, I subsided quietly. "Now then," he continued, "there are a number of things I need to attend to before I shall be ready to leave, but I expect to depart before ten in the morning. Be ready." He dismissed me with a wave of his hand.

I went dazedly in search of Mrs. Worthing and found her in the kitchen.

"What did he say to you, child?" She looked up from breaking beans.

"I'm to go to London," I replied in a trance.

"What's that?" She looked up in surprise.

"He's sending me to London to stay with some friends of his." I sat down on the bench beside her.

"For how long?"

"I don't know. He didn't say."

"Who will you be staying with?"

"I don't know the name."

Mrs. Worthing looked at me curiously. "Dear me, this is very secretive. I'll speak to the marquis and get the details."

Over my protests she transferred her apronful of beans to my lap and walked out the door. She returned ten minutes later flushed and happy. "You're a lucky child," she pronounced.

"I am?" I looked up from the beans I was disinterestedly breaking.

"Yes. His lordship said he's going to take you to stay with a very respectable widow and she will teach you how to go on. He hopes you'll make an eligible connection there."

I laughed. "No doubt he considers an eligible connection for me a wizened chimney sweep."

"Oh no, dear," Mrs. Worthing answered seriously. "Lord Linton said you were a charming girl and that it was a shame to let you wither away in this rural retreat. Those were his very words."

"He said that?"

"Yes. He likes you quite well and feels rather sorry

for you. He said there was no telling what your next wild flight would be if you were kept here."

"Wild flight!" I sputtered indignantly.

"There, there, child. Don't get excited. You're dropping the beans."

The door flew open and Janey appeared. "Forevermore, if it isn't Miss Lyons herself, back from seeing the world." She extended a handful of flowers and greenery to me. "Here."

"Thank you, Janey, they're very pretty."

"Don't be such a goose. They're not from me, they're from Jake and he's waiting outside in the garden composing a pretty speech to make to you."

"Don't look so stricken, Victoria," Mrs. Worthing consoled. "After all, you'll be gone tomorrow. Step outside in the garden and let him say his piece to you. He's been mooning about like a sick calf since you left."

I trudged reluctantly out to the garden. Sitting disconsolately on a bench, wringing his long hands together, Jake looked completely woebegone. He turned to me as he heard me approach, sprang up from the bench, nearly overturning it, and rushed toward me. "Victoria, are you all right?"

"Yes."

"Where have you been these two weeks past?"

"I was visiting a friend of my father's. We traveled a bit while I was with him. He's quite the traveler, and I only just returned yesterday." I tried to lend a little respectability to my wanderings.

"I'm so glad you're back," he said fervently, "and there's something I'm wanting to say to you."

"Not now, Jake," I coaxed. I felt guilty by his ardent and unreturned affection.

"When?"

I looked up into his brown eyes full of doglike worship and dropped my prevarication. "We can't talk at all, Jake. I'm going to be busy all day today and I'm leaving for London tomorrow and I don't know when I'll be back."

"London?" His face clouded over.

"Yes. I'm terribly sorry but, you see, I'm leaving Chilham."

"Then you won't marry me?" he stated his case directly.

"No, Jake, I'm very sorry. You see—" My explanation was interrupted.

"What about Janey?"

"Janey?" I repeated quizzically, not certain how she fit into my excuses of why I couldn't marry him. "I don't know about Janey," I dismissed her, "but the thing is, Jake, that although I like you very much I—"

"She's not going to London, is she?" he pursued.

My carefully worded refusal was forgotten in this new development. "Do you mean that if I won't have you, you intend to offer for Janey?" I asked incredulously.

"She was real nice to me while you was gone," he recalled. "If you won't have me, then she's the next one I'd want."

"I must say you're taking my refusal quite well," I huffed, offended that he was not a trifle more crushed by it.

"There's no sense crying over spilt milk," he reasoned. "Besides she's not so flighty."

"She's terribly flighty," I corrected irritably.

"She never has run away," he pointed out. "Do you think she'll have me?" He looked anxiously down into my face.

"I don't know but I certainly wish you every success," I returned sarcastically.

"Thank you," he replied, his sincerity maddening. "Then it's settled. Since you won't have me, I shall ask for her."

"Good day, Jake," I muttered as I stalked back up to the house and flung the large back door open. I walked back to the kitchen, composing myself with effort.

"Did you talk with Jake?" Mrs. Worthing asked from her position over the Rumford stove.

"Yes," I replied before turning casually to Janey. "Do you remember the time you pushed me into the creek?"

"Two summers ago?"

"Yes. And I said that I would some day get even with you?"

"I remember, why?"

"I think I just have."

CHAPTER NINE

The next morning found me preparing to travel once again. But I was making progress, I thought wickedly—Job and I had been on foot, Lord Linton and I had returned from Stonehenge in a run-down carriage, and now I was in Lord Linton's exquisite carriage.

I had taken great care with my toilet this morning, combing my hair carefully and scrubbing my face till it shone before donning my best sprigged muslin dress of a delicate ivory and my best bonnet, which was newly trimmed with ivory ribbons to match the dress. I felt quite smart, although the marquis appeared not to notice. He threw himself down in the corner of the carriage and gazed absently ahead.

The carriage jerked forward, and I was on my way to London. London! My mind was racing with the wonder of it all.

We rode along in silence for a long while, but then the very excitement became too much for me. I had to talk, even if Lord Linton's sour expression didn't seem to invite conversation.

"I suppose this is a wonderful time of year in London, being the spring and all?" I ventured.

"Yes," he returned shortly.

"Is this not the start of the London Season?" I persisted.

"Yes."

"I suppose you are all excited about that?"

"Incredibly so," he answered in a bored voice.

"Oh, but I guess it's old hat to you by now?" I continued, too caught up in my excitement to appreciate his evident lack of it.

"Why do you say that?" he queried as he favored me with a full stare from his handsome face.

I floundered. "Well, I mean, I'm sure you've been through a great many Seasons."

"Do I look as old as all that?" There was a disconcerting gleam in his eye, and I had the uncomfortable feeling that he was mocking me.

"No, of course not. I just thought, well, I thought . . . " My voice trailed off limply.

He did nothing to lessen my embarrassment. After a few uncomfortable moments he said, "I suggest, pet, that you learn to watch very closely what you say. Sometimes it even pays to think before you speak."

I hung my head in humiliation.

"Cheer up, girl. I daresay no one will notice what you say anyway. They'll be far too busy noticing other things about you." He flicked an approving look from my face to the hem of my dress and turned to stare out the window.

Thus rebuffed, I made no further attempts at light talk. We rode along in total silence, stopping only to rest the horses and once to eat. It was with relief that I staggered into the inn at Maidstone and went directly to my room to lie down and rest for just a moment. I must have dozed off and I didn't awaken until well past midnight. By then I was ravenously hungry. I laid in bed some minutes trying to lull myself back to sleep, but the very act of counting sheep made me think of roast mutton. Rubbing my complaining stomach tenderly, I finally concluded that I would have to go in search of food.

There would not be anyone in the kitchen and, circumstances being what they were, I decided to apply a little of what I had learned from Job. I crept across the room, guided by the light from the moon, and cautiously opened the door to peer out into the hall. It was very dark, almost black, but in a few seconds my eyes became accustomed to the darkness and I was able to half see and half grope my way downstairs to the kitchen.

Once inside the kitchen I found a veritable feast. By the light from the still-smoldering fireplace I could distinguish apples and pears on the table as well as biscuits and rolls wrapped in a cotton napkin. Moving as noiselessly as possible, I filled my pockets, virtuously taking no more than I thought I would eat that night, and tiptoed back upstairs. As I was entering my room, I heard voices in the room next to mine. Being naturally curious, I moved over to the door and shamelessly leaned my ear against it.

I heard a woman's voice say persuasively, "Don't be angry with me. I came because I missed you."

The voice which answered was unmistakably angry and just as unmistakably Lord Linton's. "Clarissa, have your wits gone begging? Get out of my room. What if someone were to hear you?"

"I could stay and we wouldn't have to talk," she responded in a soft, coaxing tone.

"What are you doing in Maidstone, anyway?" he demanded in a low, fierce whisper.

"I was on my way to visit you and I saw your carriage stabled at the inn," she replied. "You did invite me down, you know," she added accusingly.

"Clarissa, I must have been as mad as the King himself to have invited you. And if that was impossibly indiscreet of me, this is even more so of you. Now get out of here."

I listened in wide-eyed astonishment. Wild horses couldn't have dragged me away from his door. What did send me running was the sound of footsteps crossing toward the door I was guarding. I scurried to my room and closed the door just as Clarissa was pushed out into the hall. I listened until I heard the sound of a door closing down the hall.

I lowered myself cross-legged to the floor to eat my food absently while I reviewed in my mind the scene I had just overheard. Life with Mrs. Worthing had not exactly prepared me for events such as this, and the wonder of them kept me wide awake for some time. I finally crawled back into the bed; my last irrelevant thought before sleep overset me was to wonder what Clarissa looked like.

I awoke by degrees the next morning. After a hasty breakfast we set off again. His lordship was in no more conversational mood than the previous day, but then I hardly expected him to confide his nocturnal adventures to me. I contented myself with studying the countryside as we drove on to London.

Moving through lazy little hamlets and back out

again to the lush greening countryside, I could observe firsthand the beauties that had earned Kent the title "garden of England." It might also have been called "the place of all things wooden," I thought as we passed mansions, cottages, farmhouses, and farm buildings constructed of weather-board timber or post and plaster. There were also pretty and picturesque wooden windmills and oasthouses with conical red-tiled roofs topped with wooden cowls and wind vanes.

We passed herds of long-wooled sheep grazing contentedly in the fields. I craned my head as we passed through villages, trying not to miss anything and leaning to look past Lord Linton out his window to determine if there were some sight of great interest to be seen through it that could not be seen through mine.

Finally we came to a village that was endless. We drove down narrow seedy streets into open courtyards and then down more narrow streets. We drove past street vendors crying their wares, marketplaces, urchins playing in the streets, and men lounging sullenly in the doorways of decaying buildings.

"What town is this?" I asked, without fully intending to voice my wonder aloud.

"London, but it will be some time before we arrive at Sarah's house," he responded.

"London!" I exclaimed in a mixture of wonder and disbelief. "London."

"I apprehend that our destination has hitherto been a mystery to you," he commented mildly. "My apologies. I thought I had informed you of the object of our journey."

I turned my astonished face to Lord Linton who was lounging disinterestedly with his long legs stretched out in front of him. His green jewel eyes observed me with patent indifference from under dark fringed eyelashes.

"Of course you told me," I cried. "But that's not the same as actually being here, is it? Once, no, more than once—I should say two or three times—Papa promised that we were going to go to London and then before we could start, each time—not once but each time—something occurred which delayed the trip and so it turned out that we never went, although I have always wanted to. And now I'm here at last," I finished in breathless happiness.

"Dear me," Lord Linton murmured, "such an interesting story."

"How long will it be before we arrive at your friend's house?" I asked as soon as he had finished speaking.

"Sarah is her name, and it will be some time."

I felt some of my newfound happiness ebb away. "Does she mind very much my coming to live with her for a time?"

"No, of course not," Lord Linton replied indifferently.

"But perhaps she doesn't want to entertain someone she doesn't know," I persisted.

"She'll be glad to have you," he replied as he turned toward the window, obviously considering the conversation closed.

Suddenly I felt strangely alone. I was on my way to live with a stranger who was a refined Lady of the Town, and I wanted to be reassured that she would love to have me; but at this point of the journey it was too late to ask. If the answer was that she didn't relish having me at all, the result would be the same. I would still have to stay with her until I could find Papa. And what if I didn't find him, what then?

I was so immersed in my brooding that I didn't notice the gradual improvement of the neighborhood. When I looked up again, it was at large, spacious houses set close together. As we drove along, the houses became even larger and more widely spaced with beautiful formal gardens behind them. We passed vehicles on the street carrying occupants dressed in dignified elegance.

Finally we stopped in front of a huge brick house with high arched windows and tall white pillars across the front. I looked questioningly at the marquis.

"This is Sarah's house." A footman opened the door, and Lord Linton helped me alight.

A trim red-haired woman swept down the graceful steps to greet us. She embraced the marquis warmly.

Disengaging himself, he introduced me. "Sarah, this is Victoria. Victoria, this is Lady Sarah Hedge."

She beamed at me. "This is even better than I had dared hope. Wait until I introduce you at Lady Andover's soirée next Tuesday evening. She'll turn pea green with envy. And she has that awful-looking daughter to launch into society this year."

I curtsied, rose, and smiled uncertainly. "How do you do, Lady Hedge."

"Do call me Sarah, dear. It makes me feel not quite so old and decrepit. I'm delighted to have you. Let me show you to your room, and we can chat on the way upstairs." She motioned the footman to bring my luggage as she put her arm about me and led me up to the front door. "Wes, you know your way around," she threw over her shoulder to Lord Linton.

97

I studied my hostess covertly as she chattered excitedly about the social events awaiting me. She was an attractive woman in her early or middle thirties, slightly above average height and very slender. In a cream-colored muslin dress which was cut simply but worn with a great deal of style, she seemed more totally perfect than any woman I had ever met. Her reddish-blond hair was cut short with little tendrils of hair curling about her ears.

"I've had so little time to prepare for you. Wesley only let me know you were coming yesterday, but I do hope this room will suit," she said as she led me to the second floor and through the open door of a room which would have held the whole of Mrs. Worthing's cottage. I entered slowly and wonderingly. The walls were hung in a pink patterned paper with a dark rose rug on the floor. The furniture was a deep, gleaming mahogany. A large four-postered bed in the corner was hung with white damask curtains that matched the curtains on the long windows. In another corner was a small sitting area with dainty chairs of pink and white satin grouped around a fireplace. I walked slowly around the room, gently touching pieces of furniture or stopping to gaze at a picture. Someone said something. In a rush of embarrassment I realized Sarah had asked me a question.

I swallowed. "I'm sorry, I didn't hear you."

She smiled kindly. "I can see you're distracted so I'll leave you to familiarize yourself and we'll talk later." She left, pulling the door closed silently after her.

A pang of conscience assailed me after she left. I had been rude. After all, Sarah was being very gracious to take me in, and I certainly had not been gracious by not responding to her question. She must think me wholly rag-mannered. In an effort to correct that impression, I left my lovely bedroom and retraced my steps down the wide, curving staircase. I paused on the bottom step as the sound of voices reached my ears.

"I must say she is a very pleasant surprise," a woman's voice declared.

"What did you expect?" Lord Linton asked casually.

"Naturally I presumed she would be ugly beyond redemption. Why else would you be asking me to find her a husband? But I must tell you, Wes, even though she's beautiful, you mustn't get your hopes up too high. I promise I'll find her a husband, but I don't promise he'll be titled; perhaps a wealthy cit—someone anxious to make a connection with you."

"I don't want you to marry her off to some social climber. Just find her someone with a respectable competence."

"Honestly, Wes, have you no soul? It must, of course, be a great love match as well as an advantageous marriage. It will have to be someone who will sweep her off her feet, caring nothing for her position, or lack of it, in society."

"Don't wax so eloquent, Sarah. Just get the chit married off. She's becoming devilish uncomfortable for me."

"Why so, Wes? She doesn't look the type who would make you uncomfortable," Sarah observed.

"Well, in the ordinary way of things, that's true; however, I have now decided to become a respectable member of the nobility, and she stands fair to tempting me off that course if she remains in my household."

"What brought about this sudden reform?" Sarah's voice betrayed her amusement and skepticism.

"Actually it's not as drastic as all that. I've simply decided that it's time I settled down. Then, providentially, I inherited a country estate and it seemed the perfect time to rusticate."

"But you already had several country estates," Sarah noted practically.

"Ah, yes, but I'm well known at all of them. I can't go to Sussex or Lord Hall will have me married off to that silly daughter of his. If I go to Essex, that doddering old fool whose land marches with mine will camp on my doorstep and all my refined rudeness will not convince him that I don't wish to teach his weasel-faced son to hunt or ride. Forget the others, they have similar inconveniences. Let's just say it was easier to go to Kent."

"Except that now it too has developed an inconvenience?" There was a teasing quality in Sarah's voice.

"No, I won't allow that chit to inconvenience me any further," he stated harshly.

As I stood uncertainly at the foot of the stairs a maid walked by and looked at me curiously. Not wanting to appear foolish by turning around and going back up the stairs, I marched into the room where Sarah and Lord Linton were pursuing their discussion. Conversation ceased when I entered and they exchanged brief questioning glances before Sarah rose and came across the wide blue room to me.

"Down so soon, dear?"

"Yes. I came to say that I hope you didn't think I

was being rude by studying my room instead of attending to you," I recited dully while I tried to suppress the hurt tears that threatened.

She smiled. "Of course not. I'm sure you're worn out and excited at the same time. Perhaps you'd like to eat in your room tonight rather than come down to dinner. Later you and I can have a coze."

I nodded. "That would be very nice," I murmured, not certain whether I had committed myself to eating in my room or having a coze with Sarah.

"You go rest now," Sarah advised kindly.

I did. Later a maid brought up a dinner of fish, fresh fruit, steamed vegetables, and a strawberry syllabub. She set the tray in the little parlor corner and left. The feeling of rejection that Lord Linton's words had evoked was forgotten in the wonder of the elegance that surrounded me. I sat primly on a dainty pink-and-white striped chair and pretended to preside at a formal dinner party. Bowing and nodding graciously to my guests, I was still eating decorously when Sarah breezed in. She seated herself on a chair beside me and began to talk.

"I'm very excited that you're here. This is going to be such a good Season!" She smiled gaily. "There are a few things I need to know about you before I can start making the social arrangements. Is anyone in your family of the nobility?"

"Papa once had a dog named Duke Percival."

She smiled. "No other connections?"

"None," I admitted ruefully.

"You have lived in Kent all of your life?"

"No, I traveled with Papa until I was thirteen. I've lived in Kent since then." Deciding to make a clean breast of it, I added, "I lived on the back of Lord Linton's new estate."

"I see. Well, perhaps I should tell you something of myself. I'm a widow. No, don't say you're sorry," she interrupted me. "I've been a widow for longer than I was married and, although Tom was a good man, it was no love match. I live here with my younger sister and brother. You might have met Edward at Lord Linton's estate. My sister Maryanne did make a brief trip to Meadowacres, but I doubt that she was there long enough for you to have met her."

I tried to keep my surprise from registering in my face. I had had no idea that Sarah was Lord Lynley's sister. And if she were his sister, then she was also a sister to the girl I had met in the coach.

"Well, dear, you seem a little tired so I'll leave you to make an early evening of it if you wish." She left, still smiling merrily.

Now what? I wondered if Sarah knew that I had worked as a servant in Lord Linton's household. If she didn't, I had no doubt that her brother would make short work of informing her of it. Once she learned that information, she would see there was scant hope that I would be accepted into society, and still less that someone of the *ton* would wish to marry me. Sarah was no doubt already regretting her promise to Lord Linton to undertake chaperoning me. And just where did the marquis fit into this scheme? He had followed me all the way to Wiltshire to return me to Meadowacres and then had brought me to London with barely a breathing space between.

As I prepared for bed, the questions flitted about in my head, but I could find no clear answers.

CHAPTER TEN

I was downstairs just after the rising sun reflecting off the rose rug had painted my room a delicate shade of rose-petal pink. A maid directed me along the spacious halls walled below with oak wainscoting and above with red flocked paper to a sunny breakfast room. From a side table loaded with silver serving dishes containing ham, fish, pork, and breads of all colors, I took something of everything. I sat down at the small oval table to eat, conscientiously sampling each treat in turn. I was midway through my second plate before I was forced to lean back for a rest.

The French doors opened, and Maryanne bounced in. She stopped in surprise on seeing me, her brown eyes widening. Then she proceeded over to the side table and filled a plate. Seating herself beside me, she smoothed her amber silk gown before placing a linen napkin neatly on her lap. "So you're the girl Wes has brought from the country? What a coincidence," she noted casually.

"Isn't it?" I murmured.

"And that was not your aunt and uncle outside the inn?" she quizzed.

"No," I mumbled.

"And you are not a governess?"

"No." My voice was lower still.

"And you were not on your way to take a position in a household?"

"Er, no."

"Then I collect you were running away from Meadowacres when Ellen and I met you?"

The bluntness of her question took me aback, and I groped for a suitable reply.

"Don't waste time thinking of some polite way to answer me. You were running away, weren't you?" she demanded.

"Yes," I admitted meekly.

"Good." She nodded her copper curls in approval and continued in a friendly voice. "The first thing you have to do is assert yourself. I think you did that very well."

"I wasn't precisely trying to assert myself," I explained. "I was rather caught in a bind, and I thought I had no choice but to find my father."

Paying no heed to my words, she continued, "Your clothes, of course, are not at all *à la mode*. The first thing we must do is to be certain you are taken to the proper dressmaker. Refuse to go to Maria." She turned her large brown eyes on me and pursed her small red lips in a whisper, "She's not French, you know."

"Maria?" I repeated in bewilderment.

Maryanne chewed absently. "Yes, she's the current rage. She speaks atrocious French, although she claims to come from Calais. I rather think she's from somewhere to the south of Dublin," she confided.

"Oh." I didn't know what to say.

"I think it would be best to go to Yvette. Her tastes

104

are much more sophisticated." She tossed her head firmly. "Yes, insist on Yvette."

I nodded dumbly.

"Now then," she said, rising and motioning for me to do likewise. "I shall take you on a tour of the house."

I trailed after her as she led me out into the hall. Projecting her voice slightly, Maryanne began, "I shan't bore you with the history of the house. It's nearly two hundred years old, but it's had some extensive redecorating done to it so it looks quite modern. The last owner was a duke. He sold it to Sarah after a terrible scandal and he was obliged to leave the country."

"What kind of scandal?"

Maryanne dropped her choir director's voice to a whisper. "He was involved with another man's wife in an illicit love affair. When the woman's husband found out that he'd been cuckolded, he came raging into the house through the front door"—she pointed dramatically to the massive front door—"and said, 'Stand and deliver, ye knave.'" She struck a pose with one arm stretched forward, fist clenched.

"What did the duke do?" I prompted, intrigued.

"Well, he had been warned that the husband was coming, so he was waiting for him on the stairs, right there where they make that curve." We both transferred our gaze from the front door to the wide, graceful curve of the carpeted steps. "And the duke replied, 'I'll see you in hell, Geoffrey.'" She clarified in an aside, "The man's name was Geoffrey."

"Yes, go on," I prodded.

"Then they drew their swords and began jousting

about the hallway with each other, like so." She demonstrated by galloping around the large entry hall, fighting imaginary attackers and running a time or two at the dignified old butler, who stood watching disinterestedly.

"Who won?"

She dropped her pose and returned to where I stood. "No one," she replied in dejection. "The lady in question appeared at the top of the stairs and said, 'Jeffrey, do stop making such a scene. I shall return home with you if you will agree to give up your lightskirts.'" Maryanne fluttered her eyelashes for effect. "Very bored-like, she pranced down the steps, and the men stopped fighting. Geoffrey said it was agreeable with him if it was acceptable with His Grace to suspend the fighting. The duke, apparently never much of a swordsman, was nursing a wounded hand, and he said he was most agreeable to that arrangement."

"Then where did the disgrace come in?" I asked.

"Word of the fight was bruited aboard, and His Grace became a laughingstock, so he removed to Spain."

"Oh."

"Yes. Well, let's get back to our tour of the house."

I trotted behind her as Maryanne continued down the wide hall. She pointed to the large, well-appointed rooms on either side of the hall. We stopped at each doorway in succession to peer into the blue drawing room, the square dining room, the small breakfast room, the paneled study, and numerous smaller rooms. There was also a huge ballroom which we circled completely. At the rear the house made a right turn and extended on back to house the pantries, serving rooms, and kitchens.

After we had seen the first floor, we mounted the curling back stairs to the second floor. "These are all bedrooms and private sitting rooms," Maryanne informed me as we reached the top of the stairs and looked down the long hallway. "There are fourteen bedrooms in all. Only five are in use now—mine, yours, Sarah's, Edward's, and Wes's. I'll show you mine," she volunteered and took me down the hall to her room. She threw the door open, and I stepped into a room that was even larger than mine. It had mint-green wallpaper and drapes that were accented with silver threads interwoven into the brocade fabric. Delicate gilded pieces of furniture adorned the room.

"Everything is so beautiful," I breathed.

"Yes," she agreed. "Sarah is quite good at decorating, and all of the rooms are well appointed."

"I'm glad you showed me the house, Maryanne, but now I'd better go back to my room and unpack."

"Your maid will do that."

"I don't have a maid," I confessed with a blush.

"You do now," she giggled. "Actually Eliza has never been a maid before. She's a younger sister to Sarah's maid, but she's quite willing to learn, so all you have to do is tell her how you want things done."

"I don't know how I want things done," I answered in confusion. "I've never had a maid before. What does she do?"

"My last four have given notice after flying up into the boughs over some little thing that I said, so I'm not a very good person to ask," she admitted honestly.

"But you're the only person I know to ask."

Maryanne brightened, dropped into one of the gilt chairs, and said importantly, "In that case, the only thing a lady's maid really does is help one in and out of one's clothes."

"But I can do that myself," I exclaimed, looking down at my faded pink dress.

". . . and arrange one's hair . . ."

"I can do that myself, too," I replied and patted my hair that was tied at the nape of my neck with a pink ribbon.

"And carry excuses to callers one doesn't wish to see that milady is not at home." She wagged her forefinger at me. "That's something you can't do yourself."

"True," I acknowledged, "but you could do it for me. It seems a dreadful waste of Sarah's money to hire a maid for me."

"Sarah's not paying Eliza, Wesley is," Maryanne confided. "Sarah did hire her, but Wes told her to take care of any arrangements that were necessary for you and send him the bills."

I could think of no reply. Out of curiosity I asked, "Does Lord Linton stay here when he's in London?"

"Lord, no! He has one of the most fashionable houses in St. James's Square not three blocks from here. He's only staying with Sarah because he's having remodeling done on his house. When he arranged to have the work done he thought he was going to be in the country for some time."

"I'm to blame for his untimely return to London," I confessed. "If it hadn't been for bringing me to Sarah, he would still be at Meadowacres."

"Possibly," Maryanne agreed with her usual candor, "but then, if he was still at Meadowacres, you wouldn't

108

be in London. Besides, you won't interfere with his life. We won't be seeing much of him."

"Why is that?" I was beginning to feel that I asked a great many simple questions, but there was so much I didn't know and I felt comfortable confessing my ignorance to Maryanne.

"He's a friend of Prinny's and spends a deal of his time with that set. He also has business interests which occupy his time." She added as an afterthought, "The people visiting in Kent were there on business."

"Belinda's family too?" I asked curiously.

Maryanne smirked. "Yes, but her father was there on a completely different business than her mother. I believe her mama is now off plying her trade in Bath, trying to interest another prospect in Belinda."

"Poor girl," I sympathized.

"Yes, she's not so plain, just cowed."

A knock on the door interrupted our gossip. A shy, gangling girl appeared in the doorway. "I'm Eliza," she said in a rush, "your maid." She looked at me in awe.

I returned her look with an awestruck one of my own at the dark-eyed, dark-haired girl before me. "Hello," I greeted her self-consciously and turned to Maryanne for further instructions.

"This is Victoria," Maryanne explained to Eliza. "She's never had a maid before so she won't be hard to work for."

Eliza relaxed visibly, her skin darkening a little with a flush of relief.

Maryanne took control over her two new charges with a patronizing air. "The first thing we'll need to do is unpack clothes. Let's all go to your room, Victoria, and put your things away." As we started out the door, she called, "I'll bring along one of my dresses for you to wear today. I'm taller than you, but I don't think it will be that much too long." She grabbed a spider gauze gown from her wardrobe and followed us down the hall.

We trooped into my room and Eliza helped me into the spider gauze as Maryanne busied herself pulling dresses out of the battered portmanteau Mrs. Worthing had loaned me. "I don't see any dress that's serviceable for London," she announced when she reached the bottom of the case.

"They were serviceable for Chilham," I argued defensively.

"No doubt. But this is not Chilham and Wes wants you to look especially attractive to catch a husband. How would it reflect on him if you went about London in these rags?"

"They're not rags!" I denied hotly. "Mrs. Worthing made the dove gray one just last autumn."

"Is it dove gray?" she marveled. "I thought it was pigeon gray. Keep it," she conceded, "and give the rest to Eliza."

"But I—" began as Maryanne benevolently handed my clothes to Eliza.

"Thank you, Miss Maryanne, Miss Victoria. They're quite lovely and I shall truly enjoy them." She looked at me with honest brown eyes. "I don't think they're rags, not a bit of it."

"You may go now, Eliza," Maryanne directed. "Victoria and I are going back to my room to choose some suitable clothes for her."

I followed Maryanne back to her room, muttering

110

resentfully. "I don't think you should have given away my clothes," I informed her as she rummaged about in her closet.

"Why not?"

"Because there were some perfectly good things among them."

"Like this?" she asked, holding up a jade-colored gown of watered silk.

"Not like that," I was forced to admit as I stretched out a hand to touch it reverently.

"It's yours." She flung it into my arms. "And this." She handed me a white gown with delicate red flowers on it.

"They're lovely." The loss of my own clothes, which were definitely rags beside these, was quickly forgotten. "Surely you want to keep them for yourself."

"Whatever for? I have more clothes now than I can wear," she replied in a muffled voice from the closet as she handed three more dresses backward to me.

I rushed to the mirror to hold up the dresses one at a time in front of me.

"Are you still angry?" she asked as she emerged from the press with still more gowns.

"No!" I chirped.

"Good. Now, let's begin dressing for dinner. In one of these dresses and with your hair done right you'll be the toast of the evening."

CHAPTER ELEVEN

Maryanne was very nearly right. That evening when I appeared in the drawing room in a dark blue dress with my hair caught up on the top of my head in a cluster of curls and tied with a blue ribbon, Edward looked surprised to see me but complimented me very prettily. Sarah predicted that I would set London on its ear. The only person who appeared to be indifferent to my newfound glory was Lord Linton. He acknowledged me with a nod before offering his arm to Sarah to escort her into the dining room. Maryanne and I followed, one of us on each of Lord Lynley's arms.

Once seated at the lavishly set table, I studied the delicately painted china in confusion. Surrounding my plate were several smaller plates as well as pieces of silver and four crystal glasses. I didn't know which to use when.

Maryanne nudged me. "Watch what I do," she whispered.

I did exactly that as the painstaking meal moved along from course to course, studiously copying the pieces of silver and crystal that Maryanne used. And when she asked for a second helping of beets, I did too, thinking that it must be the proper thing to do. Sarah glanced at the pile of beets already on my plate but said nothing. Edward pretended not to notice. Only Lord Linton betrayed my *faux pas* by a smile quickly hidden behind his napkin. I blushed in humiliation and became so self-conscious I nearly overturned my water.

The meal finally ended. I rose when Sarah did, having belatedly decided she was a better lead to follow than Maryanne. We left the men to their port and went down to the drawing room, where we settled ourselves into pretty Hepplewhite chairs.

"That dress is most becoming," Sarah complimented me. "The dark blue shows your blue eyes to good advantage. We shall have several blue dresses made for you."

"That won't be necessary, but thank you. I've just acquired a whole new wardrobe." I beamed at Maryanne in appreciation.

Sarah smiled slightly. "That's very nice, dear. I'm certain that Maryanne has given you some lovely things." She cleared her throat delicately. "What I mean to say is that, although her clothes might look quite new and stylish to you, they are hopelessly *démodé*," she explained gently.

"They are?" I asked in bewilderment, looking down at my beautiful blue gown.

"Yes, dear. In London one must always be *à la mode*. It wouldn't be at all the thing to be presented in public wearing last year's garments."

I cast another uncertain look at my gown.

"I shall take you to a dressmaker tomorrow. Although it's the beginning of the Season and they're all

114

quite busy, I believe I can arrange to have Yvette fit you."

We were interrupted by the arrival of the gentlemen joining us in the drawing room. Maryanne and Edward quickly engaged themselves in a two-handed game of cards and Sarah excused herself to give instructions to the housekeeper. I shifted uncomfortably in my chair as Lord Linton walked up beside me.

"Miss Lyons, I should like to speak to you in the study," he said in very businesslike tones.

"Yes, sir," I responded meekly and followed him down to the oak-paneled study. He motioned me to an upholstered wing chair set in front of shelves of leather-bound books.

He began directly. "Since we haven't much discussed the purpose of your trip, I think we should do so now."

I had the feeling it was going to be a very one-sided discussion. I sat stiffly in the wing chair with both hands folded in my lap while he seated himself behind a massive cherry desk.

"Dear me," he said with a slight smile as he looked into my solemn face, "I feel very much like I am the headmaster and you are some incorrigible school child. You are not going to be incorrigible, are you?"

"No, sir," I returned emphatically, anxious to impress him with my amenability.

"I brought you here to meet people who may be able to help you change your station in life. Not many girls in your situation have such an opportunity, so make the most of it."

"Yes, sir."

"Follow Sarah's instructions to the letter and disre-

115

gard anything that hoyden Maryanne tells you," he lectured.

"Yes, sir."

"Now. Sarah will be buying you some clothes, hiring a dancing instructor, taking you to the theater, and so forth. Make sure my money is well spent."

"Yes, sir." I was beginning to feel like a parrot.

"I hope this show of obedience lasts," Lord Linton muttered as he rose from his chair. I also rose to leave and he escorted me to the door.

"Good night, Miss Lyons," he said before he closed the door.

Maryanne met me outside the study. "What did he say?" she whispered.

"He said he wants me to put forth my best efforts while I'm here," I related.

We turned and walked slowly toward the garden. "What he means is to put forth your best efforts so you can catch someone in parson's mousetrap and he won't have to take you back to Meadowacres," she translated. Noting my forlorn look, she consoled, "Don't worry. After all, that's why all the girls come to London for a Season—to catch a husband. So you're no different from the rest of us."

We reached the garden and strolled down the wide middle path in silence. What Maryanne said might be true; but somehow I felt different than the other girls being presented. At least if they failed to attract a husband, they had a home to go to, but I felt oddly rootless. I could only hope that Lord Linton could locate Papa before I disgraced him completely with my questionable past and silly quest for a husband. It seemed apparent to me that no man in his right mind was going to marry a dowerless girl who had worked as a servant for Lord Linton. At times I thought life on the road with Job looked better than my present situation.

I settled myself on a cold marble bench, and Maryanne left me to mope in peace. That was how Edward found me nearly a quarter of an hour later, staring up at the full moon, which was bathing the garden in soft light.

"Victoria, it's chilly out here. Perhaps you should go in."

"Yes, sir," I answered mechanically.

"Call me Edward," he smiled. Then, seeing my woebegone expression, he asked, "Is anything wrong?"

"No, sir."

He sat down on the bench beside me and began unbuttoning his waistcoat. "Then I presume you always look like you have just lost a very dear friend."

I smiled a little.

"That's better," he coached as he took his blue evening coat off and placed it on my shoulders. "I collect that Wes has discussed your future with his usual lack of tact. Actually he can be quite tactful when it pleases him to be, but I rather think he was not with you. Therefore I shall talk of your future in more cheerful terms." He leaned back on the bench and hooked his thumbs into the tiny pockets of his white satin smallclothes. "You will be attending gala balls and festivities, dancing until the wee hours of the morning, feasting on sumptuous dinners, attending the most elevating concerts, and watching some of the premier actors perform. What say you to that?"

"It will be very nice," I returned weakly.

117

He dropped his bantering tone and spoke seriously. "Actually, Victoria, it can be or it cannot be, that's up to you. But if I were you, I would dance and gossip and flirt to my heart's content. Who of the girls who arrive for the Season know when they'll be called away, by a sick relative or a father who has gambled away their dowry or a family disgrace? Yet they all arrive breathless and live with never a thought of tomorrow."

I looked up at him with interest. What he said was true, but somehow I felt the other girls were not quite like me.

He laughed and his face dimpled appealingly in the pale moonlight. "Not entirely convinced, are you? My dear, people spend their whole lives trying to make things foolproof and insulate themselves from any uncertainty. Suddenly a volcano erupts and all they have worked for is gone. Perhaps you are more fortunate than the rest; you see the volcano before it erupts."

There was something poetic about what he said, and I attempted a smile. "You are right. I shall not be so silly."

"Now you're getting in the way of it," he approved.

"Do you think I will be accepted into society?" I asked timidly.

"Of course," he replied.

"Even if I were," I ventured, considering this possibility remote, "do you think anyone would notice me in with all the pretty girls being presented?"

"Beyond standing on chairs to see you, I shouldn't think they would pay you the slightest heed," he commented dryly. Linking his arm in mine, he pulled me to my feet and we walked slowly past the carefully trimmed shrubs back to the house. His lighthearted talk had lifted my spirits amazingly and soon we were laughing together like children, and I felt completely at ease.

As we mounted the wide marble steps onto the back balcony, I turned to him gravely. "I wish to thank you for your kindness to me. I particularly wish to thank you for listening seriously while Sarah introduced me to you."

"Why shouldn't I have listened seriously? After all, she wasn't introducing the court jester." His grin in the moonlight was boyish and appealing.

I smiled ruefully. "One might have thought so when I asked for a second helping of beets tonight and I already had a plate full of them."

"You were nervous tonight. Everyone expects that."

"What I most wish to thank you for was not making mention of the fact that you had met me at Lord Linton's estate," I groped for the right words, "under rather, er, well, different circumstances."

He held the door open for me and we walked to the foot of the front stairs before he spoke. Then he took my hand and bowed over it. "Miss Lyons, I am the soul of discretion and, I trust, I am a gentleman. I should never give you cause for embarrassment." He kissed my hand in a very courtly manner.

I flushed and turned in confusion to go up the stairs. "Good night," I called back. When I ventured a look at him from the curve in the staircase, he was still watching me.

CHAPTER TWELVE

The next morning Maryanne woke me up by bouncing on my bed. "What happened last night in the garden?" she demanded when I opened one eye experimentally.

"What?" I asked drowsily.

"I saw you in the garden with Edward. Did he kiss you? Are you going to set your cap for him?"

"No. He just talked with me for a while."

"Oh," she looked disappointed, then brightened. "Well, it is something to consider. If you could fix his attention, you could easily take him down the aisle."

"I doubt that," I answered dryly, sitting up in bed. "In the first place, if he were so anxious to be married, I'm sure he would have been by now."

"He has been."

"Really? When?" I asked, much struck by the news.

"It was twelve years ago," she began dramatically. "He was twenty and Melissa was nineteen. They were married for two years and she died."

"How?"

"Her heart gave out."

"What?" I asked incredulously.

"Yes, she was always very frail, a very white-faced

thing as I recall, but then I wasn't very old at the time."

"You mustn't speak ill of the dead." I looked fearfully about the room, remembering vividly the dead woman at Stonehenge who had spoken with her son.

"Who's speaking ill? I said she was white-faced and she was," Maryanne returned practically.

"Did they have any children?" I changed the subject.

"No, which was a shame because she was so proud of her title of countess, and I think she would have liked a crowd of little lords about."

"Was he greatly overset by her death?"

"I don't remember, but I'm sure he was. Their land marched with ours and they had known each other all their lives. Yes, I daresay he was overcome with grief," Maryanne ended tragically.

The door opened and Sarah tiptoed in. Seeing Maryanne sitting on the bed, she dropped from her toes back onto her feet. "You shouldn't have disturbed our guest," she chided Maryanne. "She's had a long trip and she didn't get to her bed until quite late last night."

"I know that. She was in the garden with Edward and I'm here to find out all about it," Maryanne answered forthrightly. "I'm trying to tell her the advantages of marrying an earl right now."

"Maryanne, you will leave us for the time," Sarah commanded. "I have some things I wish to discuss with Victoria."

Maryanne danced to the door unabashed and paused to wink at me. "Remember that Edward is an earl," she called as she closed the door.

Sarah walked over to the bed and sat down on the

warm spot recently vacated. "As long as you're awake, dear, there are a few things we need to talk about." She reached over and patted my hand. "I've been doing some checking and I've found an excellent dance instructor. Your speech is unexceptional so I see no reason to hire a tutor. Where did you learn to speak so properly?"

"I was tutored by a vicar until I was nearly twelve." I thought it would be more discreet to tell just the tiniest lie rather than tell her my father had traveled in the company of a highborn strumpet who undertook the task of overseeing my education.

"Another thing," she continued, "we'll have to see about having your hair arranged, perhaps cutting it short and wearing it in curls." She craned her head around, studying my hair. "We'll see, but you can't continue to tie it back at your neck. That's much too young looking for the look of mystery I want to achieve. I intend to present you as a distant cousin of Wesley's, recently discovered. I thought perhaps a long family estrangement would make the story even more piquant. "I'll work out the details." She waved her hand airily, dismissing such petty details. "As for right now, you will be attending your first ball in two weeks, so we have lots of work ahead of us. Maryanne will be leaving next week to spend a few days in the country with my grandmama. Grandmama seems to think she is dying and that the sight of Maryanne will cheer her."

"I'm sorry."

Sarah dismissed my sympathy with another wave of her slender hand. "Grandmama's been dying for the past twenty years. It's a ploy she uses when she tires of

123

rattling about her huge Essex house alone. She refuses to come to London to spend any time with us, preferring to have us at her beck and call and dismiss us when she wishes to return to her solitude. I suppose it's a handy enough arrangement." She rose briskly from the bed. "Enough of that. I'll have the maid bring you some hot chocolate." She whisked from the room, and I laid my head back on the pillow.

When I awoke an hour or so later, I drank the cold chocolate and rose lazily. The door opened as I was attempting to don a pearl-gray dress Maryanne had given me. The tiny buttons in the back were almost impossible for me to fasten.

"Oh, Miss Victoria, you should have called me. Let me help you." Eliza fumbled with the buttons as I smoothed the front of the dress.

"Done," she announced after a good three minutes.

"Thank you." I started to walk and pitched forward onto the bed, clutching for the bed curtains as I went down.

"Are you all right?" Eliza shrieked as she yanked and tugged to help me up.

"Yes, I'm fine." I attempted to regain my dignity in front of my maid as I straightened. "The gown is a trifle long and I tripped."

"I'll pin it up," she offered, rushing to the dresser and creating chaos looking for pins.

"No, it's all right, I can hold it up."

"Are you certain?" she asked doubtfully.

"Yes. Thank you, Eliza." I started out the door and was inching my way down the stairs, holding the dress up as best as I could, when someone took my arm at the elbow. I looked up in surprise to see Edward smiling at me. I smiled warmly back at him.

"Are you just getting up? You must have worn yourself out walking in the garden."

"On the contrary, it was invigorating," I replied, looking up into his friendly face and thinking not for the first time what a handsome man he was with his friendly blue eyes and aristocratic nose all crowned by that glorious bronze hair.

"Good morning, Edward, Miss Lyons," Lord Linton startled me by speaking from behind us. We reached the bottom step as I turned to greet him. His look was cold and disdainful and I suppose he thought I was the perfect fool to come prancing down the steps on Lord Lynley's arm. He turned back to my escort. "Edward, I am going to Lord Bennington's and thought you might like to come along."

"Indeed I should. Excuse me, my dear." He bowed to me and followed the marquis out the door.

I moved on down to the breakfast room and was eating heartily when Sarah breezed up to me and took my arm. "Your dancing instructor is here, Victoria." She led me to a small room in the back of the house that overlooked the gardens. The few pieces of furniture in the middle of the room had been moved to the sides, leaving the center empty except for a fine oriental rug. Standing in the middle of the rug was a small, neat man with dark hair and a thin moustache. He bowed formally to me.

"This is Henri," Sarah introduced him.

He bowed again.

"He speaks very little English—was forced to flee France when that monster took over—but he's an excellent instructor." She turned back to the little man and smiled. "She's ready now."

Sarah walked over to a settee and sat down. A moment later she was joined by Maryanne. My attention was drawn back to my instructor as he began to give rapid instructions in a curious blend of English and French. He punctuated his directions with a great many "Do you understands?" I nodded nervously each time he asked. "Good. Now, *vous* must *simplement* do this." He executed four steps.

I hiked my gown up and attempted the four steps as he clapped his hands to keep time.

Bon. One, two, *trois, quatre*."

I stumbled.

"*Non, non*," he said nasally. "I show again."

I tried again. This time I didn't stumble, but I was hopelessly out of time.

"*Ce n'est pas* good," he intoned in grave accents.

"Perhaps we should start with something simpler," I suggested.

Maryanne giggled and Henri uttered a long stream of rapid French.

"What did he say?" I asked Sarah, turning my questioning gaze to her.

"He said those are the simplest steps there are, dear," she explained kindly.

Maryanne went off into peals of laughter.

"Maryanne, you are not doing the girl one bit of good. Go along now, she'll make much better progress without you." Sarah banished my detractor from the room.

Alas, I didn't make any better progress without Maryanne. Over the next two hours I made no very great improvement in the art of dancing and when Henri prepared to leave, his shoulders sagged slightly and he wore a look of great dejection.

"We shall see you tomorrow, Henri?" Sarah questioned him.

"*Bien,*" he replied and retreated, leaving me alone with Sarah.

"Well, dear," she said kindly. "I see we have quite a lot of work ahead of us."

"I'm sorry," I mourned.

"Never mind, I'm sure you'll get in the way of it shortly."

"Do you think so?" I asked nervously. I hated to think of myself at a great ball moving about like a rag doll to the amusement of all of society and the embarrassment of Sarah.

"Of course you will," she replied with a great deal of conviction that I hoped was genuine. "Now, why don't you go find Maryanne. I have a few notes and invitations to respond to."

I obeyed, finding Maryanne in her room, primping before the glass.

"You aren't much of a dancer," she observed as I seated myself on her bed.

"It was my first day," I said defensively.

"I wasn't that bad on my first day," she informed me as she carefully studied her face for blemishes.

"I think one reason I didn't appear to best advantage was because of the long dress," I declared, searching about in my mind for other possible excuses.

Maryanne turned a skeptical eye upon me. "You were bad, plain and simple. My advice to you is to latch onto Edward—before he sees you dance."

CHAPTER THIRTEEN

Lord Linton removed back to his own house a day after Maryanne left for Essex. That same day I was conveyed to the dressmakers amid a great deal of excitement and deposited amid oceans of materials. I knelt on the floor to finger lovingly the bolts of taffeta and silk as Sarah and the dressmaker studied me to determine the style that would be best for me.

"Stand up, Victoria, so that we can see your figure," Sarah directed. "There'll be time to look at the material later."

I stood and they circled me, stopping now and then with an "uh huh" or "ahhh" and then returning to circling. "Well," Yvette at last declared with a pleased look on her porcelain face, "I haven't had anything so promising to work with in quite some time. Most of the women I see are fifty-year-old dowagers who wish to look thirty—I am a dressmaker, not a magician," she sniffed. "Then there are the doting mamas with daughters either too fat, too thin, or too plain to work a miracle upon. Yet they drag them in here telling me to set them up in something that will cast all the other girls in the shade." She shook her head at the thought of her lot, then turned her full attention back to me.

"But this girl, with her alluring figure, raven hair, dainty features, and astounding blue eyes—her I can work with." She rubbed her hands together thoughtfully. "I think we should choose only one or two blues, they will set off her eyes but I think white will do that, as well as some rather daring shades of red and orange."

While they conferred over fashion plates, I was drawn irresistibly back to the soft materials. In colors of lavender and pale yellow, the fabrics looked like they had been spun from soft clouds. I brushed a gauze gently across my cheek, closing my eyes to savor the luxury of it.

"Victoria, we must be going now," Sarah called.

I regretfully relinquished the fabric and pattered after her to her handsome carriage, perching myself on the edge of the red velvet cushions and leaning forward to look out the window. "I can't get used to the busy pace of life in London," I enthused. "There are shops for everything!"

"Yes, there are," Sarah agreed languidly.

"Just look how smart those men are, Sarah!" I cried, pointing to two young men lounging by a streetlight and surveying the passersby with quizzing glasses.

She leaned forward to glance out the window. "Those two?" She laughed. "They're what's known as fops."

"What?"

"Dandies," she clarified.

"Oh." I felt quite stunned. They had looked magnificent to me.

"Yes, they emulate the great Beau Brummell to the

130

point of ridiculousness. We're here," she announced as the carriage pulled up in front of her grand house.

Although I had been in London well over a week, I still felt a curious surge in my stomach each time we alighted from the carriage and started into the majestic house. I had that same feeling now as we mounted the marble steps to the red brick house. The door swung open and the butler admitted us.

"Well, dear," Sarah said as she drew her gloves off and pulled her elegant bonnet off her red-gold curl. "Since Maryanne's at Grandmama's and I'm going to be quite busy this afternoon, I've made arrangements with Edward for him to accompany you to the milliners later today. In the meantime you might want to rest."

I wasn't in the least bit tired, but I retired to my room and began a letter to Mrs. Worthing. I crumpled up the third attempt at a letter and paced the room restlessly. With Maryanne gone and Sarah so busy I feared I was going to be left with considerable time on my hands.

Eliza entered as I rounded the room for the fourth time.

"Is something amiss, Miss Victoria?"

"No, Eliza, I'm just bored."

"Perhaps a turn about the garden is what you want," she suggested.

"No thanks, I've seen the garden backward and forward."

She shrugged. "As it pleases you, but walking always refreshes me." She left, closing the door quietly behind her.

Eliza was right, I decided. Walking would be just the thing. But instead of a walk in the garden, I would take a leisurely stroll down the block. There were so many elegant homes that I had only seen in passing from the carriage and this would be a perfect time to enjoy them.

I pulled on my new kid boots that pinched ever so slightly and put a sand-brown pelerine over an apricot day dress which had been altered fo fit me until my own clothes were ready. I scurried down the carpeted staircase, excited by the thought of exploring the neighborhood.

"James," I directed the butler, "if anyone asks for me, tell them I've gone for a walk."

His face took on a troubled look. "Begging your pardon, Miss Lyons, but does her ladyship know that you propose to walk by yourself?"

"No, I shan't disturb her," I called gaily as I flung the door open and hopped down the marble steps to the sidewalk. Humming to myself, I set off briskly down the street.

"Lovely morning, it is not?" a man asked, falling into step beside me.

"Quite," I agreed cheerily. "I have never heard birds sing so merrily or seen the sky such a gorgeous blue."

"No indeed," my companion replied, flicking his eyes over me briefly through a quizzing glass and then letting it dangle casually at his side. "You are new about the neighborhood?"

"Oh, I don't live in this neighborhood," I answered in shocked accents. "I should never live anyplace so grand."

His eyes narrowed slightly. "Then you are merely strolling the streets here?"

"Yes," I said and resumed humming my merry tune.

"Then perhaps you would like to return with me to my apartments to view some paintings I have recently acquired," he suggested.

"Thank you, sir, but I fear I cannot. I don't think it would be at all proper," I replied in prim tones meant to convey what an elegant and proper person I was.

"Proper?" he sneered, his wide lips curling on the word. "Since when are your kind concerned with propriety?"

"I beg your pardon, sir?" I demanded indignantly as I quickened my steps in the vain hope of outdistancing him.

"Don't play the part of the affronted innocent with me, you slut. You told me yourself you walk the streets."

I was spared any further comment when my companion was jerked roughly around by a man who had approached from behind. Turning in surprise, I found myself staring into the freezing face of Lord Linton. He was oblivious to me as he grasped my tormentor tightly by his neckcloth.

"The lady doesn't wish to be bothered by you," he snarled.

"I didn't know," the man gasped, "that she was with anyone. I thought—"

He was prevented from telling what he thought when the marquis tightened even more the grip of his cravat and growled, "I don't care what you thought. Now get out of here." Lord Linton let loose of the

133

man so quickly that he stumbled backward before turning and running as hard as he could down the street. I stood uncertainly on the sidewalk, watching his retreating form. "And just where were you going?" he demanded, turning his awful glare on me.

I quailed. "For a walk," I mumbled.

"A walk?" he asked in tones as incredulous as if I had said that I intended to run screaming through the streets. "Has not Sarah mentioned to you that it is improper for a lady to walk unattended in London?"

"She did," I admitted, "but I'm only going a short distance and this is a very good part of town, is it not? I was sure no one would accost me."

"I'm glad you approve of our taste in neighborhoods. St. James's is generally held to be an acceptable residence." His words were bitingly sarcastic. "You will not be bothered by pickpockets or thieves; however, the gentlemen of the *ton* who reside in this area can be just as dangerous. An unescorted lady is an open invitation to them. Do I make myself clear?"

"Yes," I whispered, my face reddening in humiliation.

"Good. Now I will escort you home."

Dragged would have been a more appropriate word. He banged the knocker at Sarah's house and pushed me inside as the stony-faced butler opened the door. I was prevented from running up the stairs by his lordship's firm hold on my arm. He led me into the study and slammed the door behind himself. Releasing my arm, he leaned back against the door. I cast my eyes to the floor, but I could still feel his glare burning into my face.

"You are beginning to annoy me," he said coldly.

I made no reply.

"Must someone look after your every move?"

I bit my lower lip to steady my trembling chin and studied the rug carefully.

"And don't sulk," he snapped. "I came here to discuss the progress I'm making toward finding your father, but if you continue to stand there staring at the floor, I shall leave."

"You've found Papa?" I asked excitedly, turning my hopeful eyes upward to him.

"No, I have not, but I have made inquiries of the Bow Street Runners and they are investigating."

"I see," I said in a toneless and deflated voice.

His manner changed as he motioned me to a wing chair and pulled one up beside me. "I'm sorry, child. It can't be easy to be thrust into a life amidst strangers. I'm doing everything I can to locate your father." His voice was as close to soft as I had ever heard it and I knew he meant to be comforting.

"Thank you," I said quietly, wearily thinking that his motives were no doubt highly selfish. By now he must have regretted offering me his protection and have come to the realization that I was more trouble than I was worth. Being a gentleman, the only noble way to rid himself of me was to find Papa.

He looked at me curiously, then rose abruptly. "I shall be returning to Meadowacres next week for a brief visit. If you wish to go, you may. It will only be for two or three days."

"Thank you, I should like to go."

"Very well, I shall speak to Sarah." He concluded

135

the discussion by holding the door open for me to leave.

"There you are," Sarah exclaimed as I stepped into the hall. "I've been looking for you. James was telling the oddest story about you leaving the house unescorted, but I told him you would never do such a silly thing."

"Sarah." The marquis saved me the embarrassment of replying. "I'm going to Meadowacres for a short visit next week to attend to some business matters. I thought Victoria might like to accompany me to see some of her friends."

"She cannot go back with you in a closed carriage unescorted," Sarah said in surprise. "You know that, Wes."

"That's how I came," I protested, fearful that my trip would be snatched away from me.

"Well it simply is not proper," she replied firmly. "I'm much too busy to go with you, and Eliza hasn't the experience." She looked into my fallen face. "I'm sorry, dear, but there's no one—wait. Ellen! Of course, Ellen arrives tomorrow from visiting her sister and she can go with you." She beamed at me.

I gave her an answering smile but in truth I was so daunted by the thought of being accompanied by the dragon I had encountered with Maryanne in my flight from Meadowacres that I very nearly gave up the idea of the trip.

"It's settled," the marquis declared. "We shall leave in five days."

CHAPTER FOURTEEN

Two days before my trip to Kent I prepared to attend my first ball. Henri dutifully came for my lesson, as he had every morning, but it was evident he had no great hope of a last minute miracle.

"One more time," he directed wearily as I moved to the left instead of the right for the third time in a row. This time I did it correctly. "*Bon*," he pronounced, "*très bon. C'est* all for today."

"I shall try very hard tonight," I promised him as he prepared to leave.

He gave me a look of pity before stopping to speak to Sarah. "One favor," he pleaded.

"Yes, Henri?" Sarah looked questioningly at him.

"You *serez non* tell *qui* her instructor, that is *vous ne dites—*" He broke off and looked at Sarah with pure misery reflected in his eyes.

"No," Sarah soothed, patting his arm sympathetically, "I shan't tell anyone who her instructor is."

"*Merci, merci*," he cried, bowing and nodding his way from the room.

"Now, dear," Sarah turned back to me. "We had better start our preparations for tonight immediately.

It will require the whole of the day to have both you and Maryanne ready."

Maryanne, who had arrived back from her grandmother's only the day before, was very nearly as excited as I about the ball, but not as nervous. She bounced in and out of my room as Eliza attempted to dress my hair. After two hours of pulling and yanking at it, she was kindly dismissed by Sarah, who arrived with her own maid to begin anew on my already sensitive scalp.

Finally I was ready. My hair was carefully pinned atop my head with a few ringlets cascading down my back. Sarah declared herself satisfied and hurried off to make her own preparations. Feeling like a china doll in my white chiffon dress with scooped neck and waist tied high with an embroidered ribbon that matched the embroidery on the flounces of my gown, I walked stiffly down the stairs and into the drawing room.

I peeped at myself in a glass over the mantel. One of the springy ringlets was tumbling down. I reached my hand up to tuck it back into place and disturbed another one. I jabbed at the two miscreant curls to coax them back into position, but the more I worked, the more the other curls undid themselves. In a panic I saw that more than half the curls had been knocked loose. Frantically I tried to put them back where they belonged.

Behind me I heard a quickly stifled laugh and whirled to see Lord Linton standing in the doorway fighting hard to hold back his laughter. I glared at him. Far from being chastened, he burst into peals of uproarious laughter, and it was several seconds before

138

he gained control of himself. When he did, he still chuckled softly to himself.

"I don't think it's very funny," I chirped. "We're leaving in a few minutes for my very first ball ever and I look like I just missed being run over by the Brighton stage."

"As bad as all that, is it?" I could detect little sympathy in his tone.

"I think it's the outside of enough for you to stand there and laugh," I said petulantly. "You don't have to worry about making a good impression."

"And neither do you, child. In fact, they'll like you far better if you look like you don't care what they think of you. Nothing pleases them better than to be treated arrogantly. Then they act as if you're royalty. But I can see you are paying scant heed to my words, so I had better assist you." He walked over to where I was pulling at the ringlets and placed both my hands at my sides. Then he began to pin the curls rapidly back into place, repairing me to my former glory in a matter of minutes.

"I see by that look of surprise on your face that you didn't know I was an accomplished hairdresser," he teased. Smiling down at me, he rested the palm of his large hand on my flushed cheek. I stood very still, not wanting to disturb him.

From the next room I heard Sarah calling my name. She walked into the drawing room and stopped. "Really, Wes, is it necessary to attempt innocent girls in my home?"

"Go away," he returned pleasantly without looking around. I stared in fascination up into his face.

"I will not," she retorted firmly. "Now unhand that

139

girl and let me take her out to find a man with more honorable intentions."

He winked at me. "Better do as she says. I'm no match for her, or you either to hear her tell it."

I gazed after the marquis as he departed in search of Edward. In his elegant evening clothes consisting of a black coat and pure white knee breeches he was the perfect picture of Quality. Even the easy grace with which he moved bespoke the breeding and education that was so much a part of his heritage.

I sighed and forced my attention back to the present. I saw that Sarah was regarding me thoughtfully, watching me as if she had read something on my face that I had not meant her to see. In my confusion I started to twirl a lock of my hair about my finger.

"Oh no you don't," she laughed. "Come along before you disarrange your hair. We don't want to miss a minute of this ball. Looking as you do now, you shall be the envy of every girl attending, and I am sure there is no greater satisfaction then making an entire roomful of girls green with envy."

In a few minutes Maryanne, Sarah, and I were seated in Sarah's carriage on our way to the ball.

"Nervous?" Maryanne asked as I wiped my sweaty palms on my gown for the fifth time.

"Yes."

"Don't worry," she advised sagely. "Lady Jersey or Beau Brummell won't be attending, so there's no one really important to impress."

Without meaning to spite Maryanne, I still worried. In fact, my fears increased as we mounted the wide, imposing staircase to the brightly lit house. The sound of music and laughter floated from the mansion as carriages drew up from all directions. Men, elegantly dressed in tight-fitting coats and inexpressibles, escorted bejeweled women in low-cut gowns of flowing silks and satins.

Midway up the steps we were slowed by the throng of people waiting to get into the ball. I felt at my throat and touched the simple strand of pearls that Sarah had loaned me, their cool touch reassuring me that this wasn't just a dream.

"Victoria," Sarah prompted from behind me, "do keep moving."

I obeyed, moving forward a few steps before having to stop again. When we finally reached the foyer, a footman took our pelisses, and we progressed on into the large ballroom.

An elderly woman came toward us, extending her hand graciously. "Sarah, I'm so glad you could come. And this must be your little protégée." She beamed at me. "Rumor has it that your father is a Russian count. Is that so?" she asked me.

"Yes," Sarah suppled as I stood dumb. "Victoria, this is our hostess, Lady Houghton."

I curtsied.

"Such a lovely child," Lady Houghton murmured. "Follow me, dear. I wish to introduce you to some people. You come too, Maryanne, although I suspect you already know everyone here." I followed apprehensively, darting a look back at Sarah who smiled reassuringly. Lady Houghton introduced me to at least two dozen people, most of them smiling young men. When she had completed her circuit, I was led off to dance by a tall red-haired man with a slight limp.

141

"I'm afraid I'm not a very good dancer," I offered apologetically.

He laughed, showing fine, even teeth. "Don't worry. With this limp no one will notice," he said pleasantly.

I felt my cheeks flush beet red. "I'm so sorry. I didn't mean to say . . ." I stopped in confusion.

"You didn't say, I did," he replied kindly. "Now relax, I won't eat you. If a cripple like myself can dance, a beautiful young girl such as yourself certainly can. Now smile."

I forced the corners of my mouth to curve up slightly.

"Is that the best you can do?" he coaxed. "I had a dying raccoon once named Rocky. Rocky made a brave effort such as you just have of putting on a cheerful face right before the poor creature expired." He peered at me closely. "You're not about to expire, are you?"

My smile widened.

"That's better. Now tell me all about yourself, starting with your deep, innermost thoughts."

"I shall not," I retorted with mock sternness.

"No? Well then, tell me some of Maryanne's deep, dark secrets."

I laughed. "You, sir, are incorrigible."

"You have discovered my secret," he said, pulling a long face.

"Yes, and I shall tell everyone."

"Thank you, I should be much obliged by having my name constantly on your delicate lips. I would be quite the envy of every man here."

"Gammon."

"Ah, the dance has ended, and we shall look excessively foolish if we are on an empty floor dancing without music—my limp, you know."

He led me off the floor and over to where Sarah was seated among a knot of women. I didn't even have time to sit down before two young men approached, the first leading me off to a cotillion.

Concentrating determinedly on my steps, I made little more than monosyllabic replies to my partner's questions, but they seemed to satisfy him. He returned me to Sarah with several wistful glances in my direction and a whispered compliment that I was an angel.

I doubted the man's sobriety if he could make such a statement after seeing me bumbling about on the dance floor, but I merely smiled.

My next partner was a middle-aged man with squinty eyes, and I can't remember who followed him. My apprehensions gave way to a reserved enjoyment as escort after escort presented themselves and requested a dance. By the end of the evening I was whirling about the room with a wholehearted appreciation for balls.

"This is certainly a far cry from Kent," I enthused later to the little group in our carriage. We were making our way homeward, caught in the traffic of other carriages doing likewise.

Edward had joined us for the trip home. "You were quite in demand and I heard a great many compliments about you," he praised.

"Thank you," I responded shyly. Tired and happy, I rested my head against the cushions of the carriage. "Did you have a good time, Maryanne? I didn't see you above twice all evening."

"I had a wonderful time," she rhapsodized.

"Imagine Lord Mitford asking Victoria to stand up with him a third time!" Sarah said indignantly. "He knows quite well that it is most improper to stand up with a girl more than twice."

I nodded sleepily. "He certainly looked surprised when you appeared from nowhere and sent him about his business," I giggled.

"You must on no account lose your heart to him. The man is a gazetted fortune hunter," she lectured.

"I won't," I promised. "But I shouldn't think there's anything to worry about. I haven't a fortune for him to hunt."

"Well, I'm certainly not letting that word get about. In fact, I spun such a tale for Mrs. Larston that I think she now believes you own Meadowacres. And unless I am fair and far out, she will spread that word rapidly."

Edward addressed Maryanne. "Sir Thurston seemed to be paying marked attention to you. He's quite a catch. Do you like him?"

"He has a limp," Maryanne declared as if that fact excluded him from all further serious consideration.

"He also has a fortune," Edward remarked, "which is more than can be said for Lord Stanton, whose attention you seemed to invite. Stanton's pockets have been to let for the past eleven years."

"They have not," Maryanne denied warmly.

"Did you go into the garden with Lord Stanton?" Sarah demanded. "I lost sight of you for a time."

"I would never do anything so improper!" Maryanne answered in shocked accents but a trifle too hastily.

144

Sarah pursued suspiciously. "Where were you during the cotillion before the supper dance?"

"We're home," Edward announced and the discussion was concluded as we all four climbed wearily down from the carriage and went into the house. Exhausted, I went dazedly up the stairs to let Eliza pull me out of my lovely white dress and bundle me, smiling, into bed.

CHAPTER FIFTEEN

Two days later I sat in Lord Linton's velvet-upholstered carriage with a tight-lipped Ellen and an uncommunicative Lord Linton on the road to Chilham. The marquis appeared to have a great many things on his mind and stared absently out the window as we rolled along. Ellen had favored me with one very nasty look upon entering the carriage and had then settled back in the seat and closed her eyes. To say that the conversation was stifling would be a vast understatement. After a few attempts at lighthearted banter, which met with no response, I gave up the effort and joined Lord Linton in staring out of the window.

As I watched the towns and villages go by, I savored again the delight I had felt yesterday as morning caller after morning caller had sauntered up to the house from their curricles, barouches, and carriages. They were almost exclusively male callers and, to the man, they carried bouquets of flowers. The drawing room was soon quite full of flowers, and Sarah had sent the distracted maid in search of more vases while Maryanne and I sat smiling happily and eagerly exchanging the most banal commonplaces with our current group of callers.

I felt the vehicle slow as we pulled into the yard of a large inn. We ate a light repast there and continued on our journey, stopping the night at Maidstone and arriving at Meadowacres the next day. It was with relief that I alighted into Mrs. Worthing's arms and let her lead me off into the house in a flurry of questions.

"Mrs. Worthing," I protested as I followed her into one of the grand bedrooms of the manor house, "I'm not staying here."

"Oh yes you are," she argued.

"Shouldn't I stay at the cottage with you?"

"Indeed not. You will stay here as a proper guest of milord's and not go slinking off to a back cottage. He expressly told me that you were to stay at the manor house." Her small red mouth was set sternly in her plump face.

I demurred, surprised that Lord Linton had taken the trouble to see to anything on my behalf.

"Janey has been nagging me about seeing you so I guess there'll be nothing for it but that she come up here and talk to you."

Thus announced, Janey burst through the door and greeted me with a bear hug. "Gracious, don't you look the lady in that webby green outfit?"

"It's not webby, it's lacy," I returned with dignity.

"What did you do with your old clothes?"

"I gave them to my maid," I said airily.

"Did you now? Well, I had expected you would bring me something," she hinted, digging through my portmanteau as she spoke.

148

"I'll leave you girls," Mrs. Worthing called from the doorway.

"Janey, get out of my things," I yelled lustily as she tossed them indiscriminately to the floor.

She straightened, holding a yellow chiffon overdress with a pale yellow slip. "Can I have it?"

"Where would you wear it?" I pointed out logically.

"You're being selfish," she accused.

"I am not. I simply know there's nowhere in the world for you to wear a gown like that."

"I'll wear it to my wedding," she announced slyly. "Jake proposed to me yesterday."

"I must say he recovered from the shock of my departure rapidly," I observed.

"Did you want him to pine away?"

"A little, yes," I admitted.

"Well he didn't," she stated baldly, a cheerful expression on her monkey face. Returning to the business at hand, she motioned to the dress again. "Can I have it?"

"Yes," I capitulated.

"And this lavender silk for my trousseau."

"Trousseau?" I repeated incredulously.

"It's to be a first-class wedding," she sniffed.

"All right. The silk and that's all." I drew the line firmly.

"Thank you," she bubbled. She brushed back her flyaway red hair, grabbed her loot, and rushed from the room.

Left alone, I carefully hung up my remaining dresses and laid down to fall asleep on the soft, soft bed.

I was up early the next day, eager for a walk in the

149

pleasant country air. I strolled down the lane to Mrs. Worthing's cottage, pulling at the leaves of trees as I passed and then letting the branches fly back behind me. Midway to the cottage I met his lordship.

"I trust walking unescorted in the country is not improper also?" I asked archly.

"You shall someday become a shrew," he predicted cheerfully, falling into step beside me.

"You are extremely flattering today, milord," I returned lightly. Nothing could dampen my spirits today.

"Are you glad to be back?" he asked.

"Oh yes! I didn't realize how much I missed the country until I came back." Hearing my own excited words, I thought that I must sound very ungrateful. "That's not to say that I don't appreciate you taking me to London," I added hastily.

"How did you find your first London ball? You seemed to be having a devilish good time."

I stopped walking in surprise. "I didn't see you there."

"I was only in the ballroom a short while, before retiring to a smaller room for a pastime more to my taste."

"Gaming?" I asked.

"Yes."

"You didn't even dance with me," I said in complete candor.

"No, but I shall dance with you now." He laughed and pulled me into his arms. He lifted my chin until I was looking into his emerald eyes.

"This is not dancing," I said absurdly.

150

He made no reply as he bent his lips to mine and kissed me roughly. I pulled away shaken and looked up to see him gazing at me thoughtfully. "You should not tempt me, pet. I forget that your ways are not the ways of flirtation but of innocence. Lord, it's been a long time since I've been in the company of anyone as green as you." With an abrupt change of manner, he offered me his arm. I cautiously took it, and he led me to the cottage, bowed, and left.

I paused before entering and watched him retreat down the lane. I thought how completely baffling the Marquis of Linton was. One moment he was making advances which I only half wished to discourage, and the next he was abrupt and indifferent. The problem was that while his feelings for me were only an amusement, at times I feared my feelings for him were growing deeper. With a firm resolve to erase him completely from my mind once I returned to London, I pushed the door open.

"Good morning, dear," Mrs. Worthing greeted me. "Sit down and I'll get you a cup of tea."

I sat like an honored guest in Mrs. Worthing's best chair as she busied herself about the kitchen.

"We didn't have a chance to talk about your beaux yesterday," she began as she settled herself into a chair.

"I'm afraid there's not much to tell. I've only been to one ball."

"Did you stand up with anyone?"

"Yes, almost every dance," I bragged.

"Did anyone catch your eye?"

"No, not exactly."

"There is someone," she declared, watching me with a sly smile.

151

"Well, yes. Lord Lynley, Sarah's brother, lives with her and he's been most kind to me." I paused.

"Go on," she prompted.

"He escorts me around London—he's taken me to see the Tower and all the sights. And he's very pleasant and unexceptionable to speak with . . ." I trailed off.

She watched me curiously.

"Do you know the story about the ravens at the Tower of London?" I asked. For some unaccountable reason I found myself unable to continue a discussion about men who interested me without becoming singularly depressed.

"Is there a romance?" Mrs. Worthing pressed, apparently not at all interested in raven lore.

I smiled. "You have romance and marriage in your head because of Janey's upcoming marriage."

"Janey?" she asked in perplexity.

"Yes, her marriage to Jake," I elaborated.

"Jake has been gone since three days after you left. As far as I know, Janey is not engaged," Mrs. Worthing enlightened me.

"That thief!" I expostulated, stirring my tea so rapidly that Mrs. Worthing looked at her best cup in fear of seeing it broken before her eyes. "Janey forced me to give her two of my prettiest new gowns as part of her trousseau," I tattled. "She told me she was marrying Jake."

"You've been capoted," Mrs. Worthing laughed.

I rose indignantly. "Excuse me, Mrs. Worthing. I believe I'll return to the house now."

She bid me good-bye amid a steady stream of chuckles. I stalked angrily back to the manor house and began to search for a girl in a lavender silk dress. I found her in the kitchen wearing her own old calico and trying for all the world to maintain a meek expression as I stormed in.

"Where are my clothes?" I demanded.

"In my room, but I've already altered them." Her response sounded quick and rehearsed.

"Then you can alter them back," I fumed. "You lied to me."

"You had so many new clothes and you've been to London and you have your own maid and—and everything," she complained in a whiny voice. "And all I've done is sit at this table and work the solid time you've been gone."

"I doubt that, unless you've changed your style considerably since I left," I retorted.

Janey switched tactics. "Please let me keep them," she pleaded.

"No."

"They won't fit you now anyway," she reasoned. "I'm shorter and heavier than you are.

I weakened. "All right, keep them, but don't expect me to give you anything else."

"I won't." She squirmed happily on the bench. "Now, tell me all the London gossip."

By the time Janey left that evening, I was an additional three dresses poorer. In fact I only had one gown left. She had also talked me out of one of my two new pelisses and a pair of soft leather boots. Lamenting to myself that I was ever a soft touch, I helped Mrs. Worthing set the table in the kitchen.

Lord Linton was dining with some of the neighboring gentry and Ellen had requested that her meal be sent to her room.

After our cozy repast Mrs. Worthing left for the cottage and I wandered about the spacious house restlessly. I strolled into the library and looked about for something to occupy my attention. The door of the liquor cabinet was slightly ajar, and I walked over to shut it.

On a whim I opened it instead and looked inside at the decanters of different colored liquors. I took the top off one and sniffed. It had a heavy, sweet smell—like peaches. I poured a sip into a glass and tasted it. I choked. I quickly poured some of a green liquid into the glass and swallowed it to soothe my enflamed throat. This drink had a strong mint taste and went down much more smoothly. I poured a little more of it into the glass.

"Very nice," I said aloud before tasting some of an amber liquid and then a clear-colored drink. I was beginning to feel very happy. I kicked off my shoes and tried to pick one up with my big toe. Easy. I stood on one leg and tried to hop into my shoe. I fell. Giggling, I crawled into a chair next to the liquor cabinet.

Everything felt so good. I savored another drink and then began to laugh uncontrollably over something that struck me as outrageously funny. I couldn't quite put my finger on what was so hilarious.

Bed. Time for bed. Yes. Rising from the chair, I discovered the room was like a rushing river. "Whoa," I ordered the unsteady floor. "I gotta go to . . . to bed." I lunged from the chair to the desk and across to the door over a floor that shifted constantly.

I stubbed my toe on the door. "Darn it," I muttered and limped with concentrated effort to the stairs. Reaching them, I moved slowly upward, clinging heavily to the banister. At the top of the stairs I aimed for my bedroom and lurched through the door. In the darkness I tried to unfasten the buttons of my dress but most of them eluded me. "Let go," I mumbled and with a yank freed myself of the dress as the remaining buttons popped to the floor. I stepped from it and sank into the bed, wearing my shift.

Snuggling gratefully into the covers, I bumped into something soft and warm. I cuddled up against it. The air was rent with a bloodcurdling scream and the warm spot next to me was gone. In a moment the room was lit by a wavering candle and a shaken Ellen stood regarding me incredulously. I smiled wanly up at her.

The door burst open and Lord Linton stood framed in the doorway. He was still wearing his caped driving coat and his expression was so comically puzzled looking that I began to giggle anew.

Ellen was standing in a long flannel gown with a high neck. She held a candle in one hand and pointed the other accusingly at me. "Look at her! The chit's drunk! The room reeks of alcohol." The outraged dignity in Ellen's voice and the sight of her bulging eyes were so funny that my giggles became uncontrollable.

"What's going on here?" Lord Linton demanded.

"She got into bed with me!" Ellen shouted.

Both pairs of eyes turned to me, and I felt compelled to say something. "Hi," I offered gaily.

The marquis cursed under his breath. He strode over to the bed and, before Ellen's shocked eyes, drew

155

back the bedcovers and lifted me out of the bed. Carrying me to the door, he turned and ordered Ellen back to bed, then carried me out into the darkened hallway.

In the scary darkness my laughter subsided, and I clung to him. I was on the verge of hysterical tears now. I knew he was going to throw me over the balcony to punish me for getting into Ellen's bed. I began to whimper. "I'll ne-never get in anyone's, anybody's bed again."

"Don't make rash promises, just be more discriminant," his lordship advised as he thrust open the door to my room and, pulling back the sheets with one hand, lowered me to the bed. I clung tightly to his neck.

"Let go, Victoria," he whispered. "It's hard enough to leave you as it is."

Feeling the safety of the bed, my hands fell back limply from his neck, and my head dropped heavily onto the pillow. That was the last thing I remembered.

CHAPTER SIXTEEN

I awoke the next morning with a splitting headache and a vague sense of regret. I couldn't call to mind last night's events, but I had a nagging feeling that they were not pleasant. I eased my head back onto the pillow and lay rigidly; it was the only way I could keep my head from pounding. Slowly I sank back to sleep.

I awoke again several hours later to find the sun shining brightly through the window. There was a scratching on the door and Ellen entered. The sight of her stern face regrettably brought back last night's incident clearly to my mind.

"Lord Linton says he would like to speak to you as soon as you are up," she announced grimly.

"Tell him I've fallen into a decline," I muttered.

"What?" she asked ill-temperedly.

"I'll be down in a moment." I drew a deep breath and threw back the covers. After donning a clean pink cotton dress, I brushed my hair and drew it back with a ribbon. I thought it better to go to this interview looking as sweet and innocent as possible.

Downstairs I tapped on the library door and pushed it open. Lord Linton was not one whit impressed with

157

my little-girl image. His greeting was cold and sarcastically formal. He indicated a chair and I sat down obediently as he perched on the front edge of his desk.

"Now, perhaps you would care to explain last night's drunken orgy."

"I . . . I wanted to taste them," I answered haltingly.

"From the looks of it, you certainly did that." He swept a hand toward the unstoppered and overturned decanters on the cabinet. They had obviously been kept as I left them for my benefit. I remained silent.

"And you gave Miss Marsh the fright of her life," he informed me coldly.

"I'm sorry," I said in a low voice.

"Yes, well perhaps you should tell her that." His darkly handsome face looked terribly forbidding. "Now, be so good as to explain why you felt it necessary to drink yourself into a stupor."

My voice was lower still as I repeated, "I just wanted to taste them."

"My God," he muttered. "That's the weakest damn excuse I've ever heard." He continued in a more normal voice, "I hope you learned not to mix your liquor. No wonder you were devilish foxed."

I said nothing.

"You may go now but be ready to leave for London in the morning. At least maybe Sarah can exert some control over you."

I didn't stay to be asked again. I fled the library and retired to my room to review in my mind all the tart things I should have said to Lord Linton.

My brooding was interrupted when Janey ventured

in some time later. "I hear you're in trouble with his lordship."

"Yes," I answered shortly.

"Do you want to talk about it?"

"No."

"See here, I'll give back the clothes if it will make you feel any better," she offered in a well-meant attempt to win me into better humor.

"Keep the clothes. They wouldn't make me happy now," I said forlornly and a trifle dramatically.

"What would make you happy now?"

"To have not made a fool of myself last night," I returned honestly.

"You're refining too much on it. The master has no doubt already forgotten it. After all, he has more important things to occupy his mind than the silly things a simple country girl does."

"Do you think so?"

"Course," Janey assured me as she cast predatory glances at my remaining pelisse, which I had thoughtlessly thrown over the back of a chair.

I smiled hesitantly. "Perhaps you're right."

"Of course I am. Now, show me how they dance a quadrille in London ballrooms."

I did and, in instructions best described as the blind leading the blind, we giggled and danced about the room until we collapsed in laughter on the bed.

"Sir," she giggled—I was the male partner—"your leg is sprawled most indecorously across mine. Remove it at once."

"If Henri could see me now," I chortled.

"Is Henri a suitor?"

"No," I gasped out between helpless laughter as she began to tickle me unmercifully. "My dancing teacher."

"Girls," Mrs. Worthing said severely from the doorway. "Miss Marsh has expressly asked that you maintain silence for the remainder of the day. She is indisposed and reading in her room. Come along, Janey."

Janey trailed out after Mrs. Worthing, but she had succeeded in heightening my spirits, and by the time I climbed into the carriage the following day for the return trip to London, I was almost happy.

Unfortunately my new outlook did not last past the first three miles of the journey. Ellen, wallowing in her hatred of me, spoke only when it was unavoidable and then in very clipped tones. Lord Linton ignored me as much as is humanly possible in a space as small as the interior of a carriage. Only once, when he stepped on my gown, did he glance at me as if I were anything more than the upholstery on the seat. I was still feeling the effects of my drinking bout and the motion of the vehicle was making me very queasy.

Lord Linton startled me by barking, "Are you all right?"

"Quite well, thank you," I replied with wounded dignity. I thought waspishly that his concern for me would have been more flattering if it had taken any form but its present one of a farmer looking after a runt and ailing pig.

By the time we reached London, I had decided that the entire trip was a very bad dream and I would shortly awaken. The best that can be said for it is that I didn't die; I felt so miserable that at times I wished I would.

Maryanne met me at the door of Sarah's house. "How was your trip?" she called as the marquis led me up the steps. No doubt he wished to come inside and tell Sarah how badly I had behaved.

"Quite nice," I managed to say.

"Maryanne," the marquis broke in, "tell Sarah that I have returned Miss Lyons and Miss Marsh, but that I was unable to stay. I shall speak with her later."

Maryanne nodded and vanished into the house as Ellen edged past me, casting a hateful sidelong glance in my direction.

I took a deep breath of air and turned back to Lord Linton. "Thank you for taking me. I'm sorry I was so much trouble to you."

His eyes flicked over me coldly. "You are quite welcome, Miss Lyons. I bid you a good day." He shifted his coat more firmly on his shoulders and descended the steps back to his carriage.

I went into the house to be engulfed in Sarah's arms. "How was your ride, dear? You look so very tired."

"I am a trifle worn out," I confessed.

"Go to bed and you can tell us all the details later." Maryanne followed me up the steps, chattering excitedly. "We both had gentlemen callers."

"Who?" I queried.

"Lord Stanton called on me twice," she related dreamily.

"Who called on me?"

"And the red-haired man with the limp, Sir Thurston, called on me twice. Then Mr. Adams stopped by, but I rather think he was more interested in Sarah than in me—he's quite forty you know."

"Who called on me?" I asked patiently as we

161

reached my room and she leaned against the wall. "After that I had a surprise caller. Guess who it was?"

"I don't care," I wailed. "I want to know who called on me."

"Well don't fly up into the boughs about it," she advised in a reasonable tone, as if speaking to one who is slightly unhinged. "I'm coming to your callers—one was a dandyish fellow, can't recall his name; then a fat man with large red spots on his face; and then a grandfatherly gentleman."

"Is that all?" I asked in disappointment.

"No. There were quite a few young men, but I don't recollect any of their names just now. Ask Sarah."

"I shall," I returned, piqued that she had in no wise satisfied my curiosity.

"Well, don't be in such low spirits. I have some good news for you. Ellen is leaving."

"She is?"

"Yes, her sister has sent for her again. And Edward is leaving too."

"Where is he going?" I asked in surprise.

"To our family estate in Sussex. It's where I lived until our parents died. Every now and then Edward decides he's going to be an improving landlord and returns to Forestview. A short visit usually convinces him that the estate is managed very competently without him and he returns to London. Edward prefers White's and Crockford's far too much to rusticate long in provincial Sussex."

"Who are the Whites and the Crockfords?" I asked.

Maryanne regarded me with unholy amusement written on her appealing little face. "Not who," she corrected me, "what. They're gaming houses."

"I didn't know that," I answered honestly.

"I think there are a great many things about gentle-men you do not know," she pronounced wisely, "but I shall teach you."

CHAPTER SEVENTEEN

During the next week Edward left for his estate in the country and Maryanne and I prepared for the biggest event of the Season.

The Bridgewater's ball was a glittering affair. Women came in diamond and emerald tiaras wearing exquisite flowing gowns cut very low to the bosom and carrying elaborate little fans. The men wore expertly folded cravats, superfine coats, and tight-fitting breeches of all colors. They moved about in a very neoclassical room with arched windows, Doric columns, and lavish ceiling moldings. Life-size nymphs danced about the wallpaper, and there was a lavish fountain in the center of the room.

I arrived wide-eyed with Sarah. To my utter disbelief Maryanne had pleaded a headache and remained at the house. Although I had assured her that I would not enjoy myself at all knowing that she was suffering, I soon forgot my resolution in the excitement of the evening.

I danced with so many young men, my feet were becoming numb.

"Are you feeling quite the thing?" Lord Mitford asked. I was limping through a quadrille with him.

"No, I shall drop if I take above two more steps," I confided.

"There's no need for such drastic measures. Here's the end of the dance now." He led me over to a corner seat wedged in between a pillar and a large palm plant. "No one will find you here. I'll procure you a refreshment," he offered and disappeared into the crowd.

While I waited for him to return I fought off the advances of the invading fronds of the palm. They dipped down toward the chair and there was no way I could sit that they didn't brush against my face and disarrange my carefully coiffed hair.

"Who's winning?"

I looked up into Lord Mitford's amused face. "I'm afraid the plant is," I admitted.

"Then what say we forgo the ratafia—there's a huge crowd around the refreshment table—and take a stroll in the garden? Who knows, they may have more and larger palms outside."

"I don't think I should," I hesitated.

"Why not?" he parried.

I studied the tall man before me. He had piercing eyes and a rather short Roman nose, but he was handsome. He had called twice at the house and had been paying marked attention to me this evening. Surely there could be no harm in sniffing a few flowers with him in the garden.

I smiled encouragingly and rose, taking his proffered arm, and walked with him out the open doors onto the balcony and down the tile steps to the darkened garden. We followed a path through the garden to the back, never once stopping to look at the flowers, although I suggested it a time or two. At the back of the garden he led me into a small building—it was only one room, lit with wavering candles and furnished with a massive Chippendale desk, some chairs, and a settee. He drew me toward the settee.

"Should we be here?" I asked worriedly.

"Of course. The door was open and the room lit. When one has a party, it is expected that one's guests will peep into all sorts of closed rooms and dresser drawers. An open room is an invitation for people to pry."

While I assimilated the logic of that, he pulled me down beside him on the settee. "Actually, this is where George Bridgewater writes. He fancies himself a great poet and has the room open day and night on the off-chance that he should be greatly inspired and want to come running down here to dash off an ode or a few sonnets." Lord Mitford rose and went to the desk, pulled open the top drawer, and extracted several sheets of paper. "Here's his latest effort:

> Your life is like the silver moon,
> That floats across the sky,
> Yet vanishes, alas, too soon,
> and leaves me here to die . . .

What do you think?" he asked.

"I think we shouldn't be disturbing his personal things, especially not something as sacred as his attempt to put his feelings into words," I replied honestly.

167

He gave a short, unpleasant laugh. "George has no feelings. These sorry poems are the feeble attempt to create some. He's just an aging dandy who has nowhere else to fix his interest."

I was beginning to feel distinctly uncomfortable. A man who had no regard for another man's feelings was not very likely to have any for mine. I was thinking of some clever way to persuade him to take me back to the ballroom when he suddenly closed the door and crossed the room toward me.

I jumped up and sidestepped neatly around a chair. I clung to the back of the chair as I regarded his amused face haughtily.

"I'd like to lessen the distance between us," he said persuasively as he took a step closer to my defense line. "I really like you, Victoria."

"It's Miss Lyons, and I am certain you overestimate your feelings for me," I replied in tones meant to give him a sharp setdown.

"You looked like a goddess on the dance floor," he purred.

"I'm not at all a good dancer," I objected.

"My dear, I can stand up with any chit, but it is very few women who affect me as you have." He had reached the chair and was edging around it as I retreated backward to the wall. Stopped by the wall, I watched him advance, smiling smugly. He halted in front of me and put a hand on the wall on either side of me. Casually he shifted his weight to one foot and leaned slightly forward. "You are so pretty," he whispered.

"I don't think we should be here," I informed him in an arch manner I was frankly copying from Sarah. I hoped I sounded as intimidating as she did when she applied it.

Evidently I didn't because Lord Mitford merely shrugged indifferently and smiled tolerantly at me.

"If you do not let me leave, I shall have to use force with you," I said severely.

"I should rather enjoy the physical contact," he replied, evincing no real fear of me. "I fancy you're quite a pugilist, although not in the usual Gentleman Jackson style." His smile was sensual and amused.

Putting both of my hands on his shoulders, I tried to push him away. His smile widened perceptibly at my ineffectual efforts. Angry now in good earnest, I kicked with all my might the leg supporting his weight. As he stumbled and grasped his leg, I dashed madly for the door. I jerked it open, nearly colliding with a pair of entwined lovers, and pushed past them with incoherent apologies. I scampered back up the steps to the balcony and into the ballroom.

I was standing panting in the doorway, looking rapidly about for Sarah, when I heard a voice at my elbow. "Miss Lyons, you must do me the honor of dancing with me." So saying, Lord Linton took me into his arms and we danced out onto the floor in the middle of the set. "Now, Miss Lyons, just act naturally, as if nothing had happened."

I peeped up into his face warily.

He continued smoothly. "Stop wasting those devastating looks on me; it is quite obvious that you have just come from a very intimate meeting with some young swain."

"Why do you say that?" I asked timidly.

"Please, Miss Lyons, I'm well past my salad days,

and I'm enough of a man of the world to know that, when a young lady leaves in the company of a gentleman and returns alone—wild-eyed and with her mouth gaping, looking for all the world like a frightened cow—all did not go well."

I blushed, as much at his description of me as for my actions. He had spoken low to my ear, but I glanced around apprehensively to see if anyone had overheard.

"And it's a trifle late to be wondering what people are thinking," he continued. "You should have thought of that before you went sneaking off into the garden. Now, I believe we should pay our respects to the hostess and I will escort you home. It's early to be leaving, but I fear if we stay, you shall not be able to carry this little event off without giving yourself away."

Sarah seemed surprised when Lord Linton collected her and explained that he would escort us home. I added helpfully that I was fatigued and wished to go.

"All right, dear," she murmured before saying her good-byes to her circle of dowagers.

Inside the carriage little was said. Sarah looked questioningly from the marquis to me but made no inquiries. When the carriage pulled up in front of the house, Lord Linton helped her alight and then held out his hand for me. He retained his grip on my arm and escorted me up the steps to the house and into the study where he closed the door and stood watching me quizzically.

"In the future do not go unescorted with men into dark places." His face reflected controlled amusement.

As I watched in amazement, he smiled a disarming smile. "Did you expect me to be angry?"

I nodded.

"Well, my captivating blue-eyed doe, you have very little experience and how were you to know for certain that men are not to be trusted? I'm certain that he fed you a very pretty and convincing line, and you were too green to be distrustful. Of course, you did have your first meetings with me to judge by, but perhaps you have forgotten them in the swirl of London life." He stretched out a hand and lightly pinched my blushing cheek before turning to the desk. "I must leave a note for Edward. Good night."

I was obviously dismissed and yet I lingered. He looked up from his task of filling the pen with ink. "Yes? Is there something further?"

"No, sir, good night," I answered meekly.

I reflected on the way upstairs that it was odd that two men could affect me so differently. After all, Lord Linton and Lord Mitford were both good-looking, elegant, charming (when they chose to be) men. Why then was it an annoyance for one to show attention to me and an annoyance that the other one didn't. Before tonight Lord Linton had never even danced with me. I caught myself on the top step. Was I really annoyed that the marquis didn't show any interest in me beyond that of an incorrigible flirt and a guardian? Yes, I had to admit, I was. A second voice inside me said severely that there was nothing to be gained by his attentions as he was obviously not going to fall in love with and marry a girl he had brought all the way to London expressly to marry off to someone else.

171

"Pssst, come here." Maryanne was whispering to me through a crack in her door. She held the door open wide enough for me to squeeze through, then closed it quietly. "You certainly made a thorough study of the carpet on that last step. I thought you had gone into some sort of trance."

"What do you want?" I asked pointedly. I wanted to sort out my thoughts and I was in no mood to talk.

"Heavens! Don't try to cozen me with sweet talk. Why did you come home so early?"

I ignored her question and countered with one of my own. "I thought you were deathly ill with a headache."

"Quite a miraculous recovery. I'm sure it will be in all the medical journals," she answered glibly. Becoming suddenly serious, she continued, "Was Lord Stanton there? Did he dance with you? Did he ask about me?"

"Two yeses and a no. You may place them wherever you please."

"You certainly are odious tonight. Did you commit some sort of dreadful *faux pas?*" she interrogated. "Is that why you're home early?"

"Yes," I sighed, sinking into a gilt chair. "I did commit a *faux pas.* I left the dance with Lord Mitford and he took me out to a secluded room in the garden."

"What happened?" she asked breathlessly.

"Nothing."

"How very disappointing. No wonder you left. I hoped he had proposed."

"Maryanne, I don't mean to sound rude, but please don't be obsessed with finding a husband for me. Every man who has come to call, you have made grandi-

172

ose plans for—even with two who are old enough to be my father. Why do we not let nature take its course and if someone comes along who wants to marry me, they will no doubt ask."

"What if the right person doesn't come along?" she questioned.

"Then you cannot force anything to happen," I replied practically.

She flopped down on the bed and rolled onto her back. "I think you are right. I cannot force the issue, but just for conversation's sake, what did Lord Mitford say to you?"

"He read me poetry and swept me into his arms."

"Oh, that's rather conventional, isn't it?" She sounded disappointed.

"What did you expect him to do?" I demanded irritably. "Besides it didn't happen in just exactly that light."

"I would want a man to do something very daring to win my love—perhaps swim the Channel."

"Then you would end up married to a man with shriveled-up skin," I observed unromantically. My curiosity aroused, I asked, "Why did you feign a headache tonight? Especially if you wanted to see Lord Stanton?"

"Because if I had been there, he would have danced a time or two with me as well as thirty other girls. This way I have the distinction of being the girl he did not dance with." Her voice took on a dreamy quality as she continued. "I will be surrounded in his mind's eye with a cloud of mystery. Tonight as he loosens his cravat, he will muse, 'But why was Maryanne not there? Perhaps she is quite ill.' He will take

173

off his shirt and sit on the bed to remove his boots. 'I should go to see her. It is possible that silly Victoria did not tell me the whole of it when I asked after darling Maryanne.' He will lean against the rail of the bed and think, 'Sweet Maryanne, not at all like the fast young women one meets today, more like a pure goddess of yesteryear. I must see her tomorrow. She may be ill indeed.' "

I made a short little noise that adequately conveyed my sentiments about her melodrama.

"And then his last act will be—"

"I don't care if it's the first act of *Hamlet*. I'm going to bed."

CHAPTER EIGHTEEN

Edward returned from Sussex the next day and brought a small dog for Maryanne. It was a spry, gray-haired little creature with very sharp teeth. Its first act once inside the house was to exercise its teeth emphatically on my hand.

"Ouch," I squealed and grabbed my hand back.

"Poor Doggy," Maryanne soothed him. "He's scared."

"Poor Doggy? What about me? I'm injured," I announced hotly.

"Please, girls," Sarah interrupted our bickering. "Maryanne, take the dog away for a while."

Maryanne scooped up the dog and carried him off protectively to her room. We exchanged glares as she passed. I nursed my bitten finger for a few minutes and then began to ascend the stairs to my own room.

My attention was caught by a short cracking sound. I stopped in the hall and listened. The noise came again. My curiosity aroused, I followed it to a small room down the hall and peeked in a half-open door. The room had red velvet drapes and dark wood paneling. There were a few chairs upholstered in velvet that had been pushed back against the walls. In the center of the room was a big, rectangular table. Edward was walking around it holding a long stick. He stopped occasionally and aimed the stick at one of several balls on the table. He was so absorbed in his game that he didn't notice me. I ventured up closer.

Edward looked up and smiled. "Just arrived today. What do you think?"

"What is it?" I asked uncertainly.

"It's a billiard table. I've been wanting one for some time. Look at this—inlaid mahogany." He pounded the side of the table with an appreciative grin.

"It's very nice. What do you use it for?"

"The object of the game is to get these ivory balls in those little pockets. You shoot like this." He demonstrated.

"You mean all you do is shoot those balls in the pockets?"

"Yes. Off of this ball," he indicated by tapping a ball with the stick.

"It looks easy." I regarded the table in perplexity, failing to see the challenge of the game.

"Of course it looks easy," he replied, affronted. "Everything looks easy when someone else is doing it. Here, try it." He waved the stick at me.

I took the stick and started to shoot.

"No, no, not like that. Here, hold the stick like this, like so." He maneuvered the stick around in my hands. "Now, place your hand like this on the table, stretching your finger around here." He pried my fingers into position. I felt like a contortionist. "Now shoot," he commanded.

I shot and missed.

"Not as easy as it looks, is it?" he asked with more than a hint of satisfaction as he held his hand out for the stick.

"Just a minute, please." I moved the stick around in my hands to my original position and shot. There was a cracking of balls hitting each other and then a dull thud as a ball fell into a pocket. Edward ran his hand briskly through his curly red hair in astonishment.

"Try again," he prompted.

I moved around to the other side of the table and lined up with another ball. I shot and it, too, dropped into a pocket. Greatly encouraged, I aimed for a ball lying up against the rim of the table. I barely tapped it and it rolled to the edge of a pocket and stopped.

Edward gave a long, low whistle. "Are you sure you haven't played this before?"

"No, but I rather like it," I returned honestly.

"Try again."

Over the next two hours we took turns shooting at the balls. In all honesty, I must confess that I was much better than Edward. He made a respectable number of his shots, but I made well over three quarters of mine. We were finally forced to stop when guests arrived to visit.

At dinnertime I was about to descend the stairs to the drawing room when the door opened and Lord Linton was admitted. I stopped and watched him furtively as he entered with an easy grace and tossed his hat to the butler. Edward emerged from another room and clapped him good-naturedly on the shoulder.

"I received your urgent message to come for dinner. What's amiss?"

"Nothing whatever," Edward returned blandly. "I merely have a new toy and I wished you to try it out."

"Really, Edward," Lord Linton said in an amused voice, "one of the ladies might overhear you. What's her name?"

"That's not what I meant," Edward replied affably. "It happens to be a billiard table—far superior to yours, I believe."

"That sounds remarkably like a challenge to me." Their voices faded as they proceeded into the drawing room. I followed after a brief interval, and we shortly removed to the dining room.

After a leisurely dinner Edward suggested, "What say we forgo the port, Wes, and have a game or two of billiards? Perhaps the ladies would like to join us."

"Of course," Lord Linton agreed lazily.

We adjourned to the billiard room where the marquis surveyed the table critically before pronouncing it passable. Maryanne and Sarah settled themselves into the red velvet chairs, suppressing sighs of boredom, while I rested the palms of my hands on the table rim and watched with interest.

"What do you make of a table with holes in it?" Lord Linton asked me casually.

"Oh, this afternoon I—" I began excitedly.

Edward interrupted swiftly, "Are you cold, Victoria? Do you need a wrap?"

"No," I answered in surprise. "I'm not cold. It's quite warm in here."

"So easy to take a chill on these spring evenings," Edward continued smoothly. "Take a practice shot, Wes."

The two men took a few practice tries and then began to play in earnest. It was a mismatched game, Lord Linton beating Edward by several balls.

When Lord Linton offered to play again, Edward declined. "Perhaps one of the ladies would like to play," he suggested nonchalantly.

"I don't think they would be interested," the marquis returned in a bored voice.

"Victoria appears interested," Edward suggested wickedly as he rapidly lined up the balls for a new game.

The marquis shot a look of exasperation at Edward but resigned himself to a game with me as there appeared to be no graceful way out. "Ladies first," he smiled benignly at me, handing me the stick.

"Wait," Edward interrupted. "Just to add some interest to the game, what do you say we make a little wager?"

"Edward," Lord Linton began impatiently, "it would hardly be gentlemanly of me to play for stakes against an amateur like Victoria." He turned to me again. "Go ahead, my dear."

I started to shoot again.

"Really, Wes, if Victoria is willing, I should think you would have no objection," Edward pursued.

"Victoria has not said that she is willing. Besides, I can't take her wager on a game she will most certainly lose," Lord Linton snapped with unguarded annoyance.

Poised over my shot, I felt defiance flow through me. Straightening, I turned to the marquis. "No, I believe Edward is right. A wager would make the game more interesting. I insist on one."

179

"And just what would we wager?" Lord Linton asked caustically.

Edward supplied quickly, "If Victoria wins, you buy her a horse; if you win, she will monogram you a set of handkerchiefs."

Lord Linton gazed at Edward as if he had taken leave of all of his senses.

"I hardly think that's fair," I interrupted. "A horse against handkerchiefs is not a balanced wager. Besides, I don't want a horse," I ended emphatically.

Mitford transferred his stare of disbelief to me. "Have you people run mad? Let's just get this silly game over with instead of arguing over who will wager what; I scarcely see that it matters. For the sake of halting this pointless argument, we will let Edward's suggestion stand. Now shoot, Victoria."

I shot with barely enough force to scatter the group of balls.

Edward smiled and Lord Linton patted my arm. "You'll get in the way of it," he offered kindly. "I daresay you'll catch on fast."

Over the next several minutes I caught on a trifle too fast for Lord Linton's comfort. When my first ball dropped into the pocket, he looked slightly surprised, but when the next three followed rapidly, he appeared to go from surprise to an angry acceptance that he had been foiled.

Maryanne and Sarah rose from their chairs and came over to the table to watch with interest. Edward maintained a sardonically superior grin as Lord Linton's face became more and more flushed. In the end, I won.

180

"Congratulations, my dear," the marquis said tersely. "I fear I must depart now." He stalked out the door and down the hall. I followed, feeling very guilty and devious. As the butler handed him his curly brimmed beaver hat, I searched for something to say.

"Don't forget Victoria's horse," Edward called from down the hall as the door swung open and Lord Linton stormed out.

CHAPTER NINETEEN

I meant to write Lord Linton a note the following day apologizing for the previous night's events, but morning callers prevented me from doing so. We were visited by several smiling young men as well as one or two past the young stage. We sat in the drawing room and, since I wasn't certain which ones were there to see Maryanne and which ones to see me, I smiled indiscriminately at them and directed most of my conversation to no one in particular.

Maryanne's two definite conquests did make an appearance near the end of the morning. Her brown eyes lit up when Lord Stanton entered the room and her chatter doubled in vivacity. Sir Thurston arrived a short time later and, although he did not cast her into an equal amount of transports, she was civil if not encouraging to him. He seemed to take it in good part that she showed no marked preference for him, limping into the room and nodding agreeably to all present before settling down to talk to Sarah until he could draw Maryanne's attention.

By the time the house was cleared of callers, it was well past noon and Maryanne and Sarah rushed off to a fitting. I was on my way upstairs when Lord Linton arrived.

Spying me in the hall, he tossed his riding crop and hat to the butler and crossed the room to where I stood. "I have your horse," he announced abruptly.

I blushed. "I didn't mean . . . that is, I—" My stammering was interrupted by the sound of Edward's voice calling heartily down the stairs.

"Ah, such a fine day to go visiting, don't you agree, Wes?" Edward halted in front of us and smiled cheerfully into Lord Linton's stony face. "Really, Wes, you're not going to be a bad sport, are you? Victoria did win fairly, you know."

"I was tricked," the marquis replied tersely.

"Assuredly, but I thought you would see the humor of it today. Anyway, don't be angry with Victoria. She wasn't a party to it."

Lord Linton glowered at Edward, who maintained his sunny smile in the face of all adversity, before giving a short laugh and clapping his hand on Edward's shoulder. "You're right, I'm acting like a coxcomb. I concede defeat." Turning to me, he smiled, his green eyes twinkling. "Now, I have just purchased an excellent bay mare after spending a morning at Tattersalls. And whilst we argue in here, said horse is waiting outside in the heat. Shall we go have a look?"

"I can't accept a horse. It wouldn't be proper," I protested.

The marquis took my arm and steered me to the door. "Oh yes you'll accept a horse. I won't have my morning wasted. It's high time you had one anyway and, aside from winning the horse in a fair wager, I am your guardian and it is my duty to provide such things for you."

As the butler held the door open, Lord Linton led me out and down the steps. Edward had preceded us and was giving the horse a thorough check-over. The bay tossed its head sharply, and I took a hasty step backward.

I should have felt gratitude and pride, but instead I found myself wishing I had contrived to lose the billiard game last night. I had been on horses before—Papa had had a horse for a short time and he had carried me around with him when I was only seven or so—but that is not precisely the same as riding one by oneself. And this creature was too big, too angry looking, and had a seat far too high off the ground.

I walked around to look at the mare's face while Lord Linton discussed the finer points of her with Edward. Large brown eyes stared back at me contemptuously. "It doesn't like me," I said, backing away a step.

"What did you say?" Edward asked.

"This horse doesn't like me," I repeated.

The men exchanged looks and came around to the horse's head. "Why do you say that?" Lord Linton asked.

"It's giving me an evil look."

"Haven't you ever ridden before?" The marquis looked at me curiously.

"Only a few times and never alone. Papa had a horse a short while; there was some dispute over the horse's true ownership and the magistrate took it away from us. But even when we had it, I never rode by myself. I don't like horses," I ended forlornly.

"I'll teach you to ride," Edward offered kindly.

The marquis looked at him sharply. "Nonsense, Edward, Victoria is my responsibility and I shall teach her to ride."

"Wes, you don't have the patience for that type of job. In a week she'd be even more frightened of this mare than she is now. It won't be any trouble. We shall go every morning to the park before anyone is about," Edward announced, then turned and mounted the steps into the house.

Lord Linton bid the waiting groom take the horse to the stables, wished me a good day, and took his leave.

The following morning found me reluctantly in Hyde Park. Edward and I walked the horses to the park and then he helped me mount. Looking down from my perch, I thought bleakly what a long way it was to the ground and prayed fervently that my next encounter with that ground would be feetfirst.

"Now, Victoria," Edward was saying, "hold the reins like so and pull this way to make her turn. Do you see?"

I nodded nervously and tried to do everything exactly as he had said, but when the horse began to walk faster, I panicked and jerked back fiercely on the reins. The horse reared its head back and neighed loudly.

"I want to get off!" I pleaded.

"Now, Victoria, you must let the horse know who is in control," Edward counseled calmly from beside me.

"She knows! She knows! Let me off," I cried.

Edward dismounted from his horse and helped me down. "I'll tell you what. I'll tie my horse up here and ride with you for a few minutes. That way you can get used to being off the ground as well as feeling the motion of the horse."

"I want to be used to being on the ground," I wailed. "I like being on the ground." Struck by a sudden thought, I grabbed the impeccable lapels of Edward's brown riding coat and cried, "Edward, listen to me. We'll sell the horse! We'll tell Lord Linton that she ran away—we tried to catch her, running after her through the park, but she was too fast—yes, that's it, she ran away. So, as much as I wish to, I won't be able to take any more riding lessons." I looked up anxiously into Edward's face to see how he was receiving my suggestion.

"Victoria, pray control yourself," he said sternly. "Are you ready to try again?"

I bit my lip and nodded tremulously while Edward tied his horse to a tree and mounted my bay and pulled me up behind him. I was seated in the sidesaddle and he was riding practically on the horse's neck. He handed the reins around to me, still keeping a gentle hold on them, and showed me again how to manage them. The security of having this strong man with me gave me encouragement. I was concentrating very hard on maneuvering the reins when a voice beside me startled me.

"I bought the horse for Victoria, not for you, Edward," Lord Linton drawled, pulling up beside us on a magnificent black stallion.

Undaunted, Edward laughed. "I intend to sell my horse, and Victoria and I shall ride about London like this. It will save me the cost of feeding and stabling an extra animal."

187

"How goes it?" Lord Linton transferred his attention to me.

"Not very well, I'm afraid," I returned truthfully.

"You'll get in the way of it soon enough. Edward, why don't you get off of there. You make a ridiculous sight."

Edward slowed the horse and leaped down. Left alone once again on this moving mountain, my fear began to rise.

"Victoria," Lord Linton was saying quietly, "hold the reins like so." He leaned across from his stallion and placed the reins more firmly in my nerveless fingers, then whipped slightly at the horse's flank and urged her to a faster pace. I clung on bravely, praying for the end of the lesson.

It came mercifully an hour later.

"You've made progress today," Edward commented as we walked back to the house. Lord Linton had left a quarter of an hour earlier, bidding me not to despair.

My legs felt oddly unsteady on solid ground. "Perhaps we shouldn't rush the lessons," I suggested. "It wouldn't pay to overdo it."

"What did you have in mind? One lesson every other year?" Edward inquired in an amused voice.

"Something like that," I admitted.

"No, my girl, we're going to be in the park every morning until you have a good seat and can manage the reins expertly."

"Then I'm very much afraid we shall be there when I'm one and ninety."

"Have no fear. I shall enjoy escorting you as much then as I do now," he replied gallantly. "In fact if you continue to wear that fetching green velvet riding costume with that provocative little hat, half the men in London will be spending their mornings in the park."

"Do you like the outfit? It's not mine. Maryanne loaned it to me."

"Advise Maryanne to loan you all of her clothes as she cannot possibly do them the justice that you do them."

I blushed shyly at his compliments but continued to savor them all the way home. We mounted the steps to the house just as Maryanne and Sarah were leaving with the dog.

"Victoria, do you wish to go for a walk with us?" Maryanne asked. The dog bared its teeth at me.

"No," I declined hastily. "I have several things to do."

Actually I had nothing to do. I wandered slowly to the garden and sat down on a marble bench by the rows of rose bushes. I was idly shredding a flower when I heard a noise down the path. I glanced up disinterestedly but didn't see anyone. Then I froze. The rose bush down the path was talking! It was whispering, "Come 'ere," in a throaty voice.

I stood up shaking, remembering vividly all the ghost stories I had heard as a child, and edged around the side of the bench, backing away from the bush.

"Listen, lassie, I'm not on fire and you're not Moses. Now git over 'ere right now." The voice was imperious but had an oddly familiar sound to it. I moved timidly forward. "Come around to the other side," the voice continued, "so's we can't be seen from the house."

I obeyed hesitantly. Peering over the bush, I spied a

man crouched behind it. "Job!" I exclaimed, "what are you doing here?"

"Quiet," he commanded. "Do you want them to set the dogs on me?"

"But what are you doing here?" I persisted.

"I've come to take you to your pa."

"Papa!" Flustered, I moved first in one direction, then in another. "Let me get my reticule and I'll be right back."

Job stood up swiftly and grabbed my arm. "Listen for a minute, will ye? I'm not takin' you now. I'll come for ye tonight and no one kin know where you're goin'. Do ye understand?"

"No, what's wrong?"

"The Bow Street Runners is alookin' for your pa. They think he was mixed up in a house that was broke into and robbed 'ere a couple of nights back."

"Oh no! Papa would never do a thing like that," I declared, aghast at the misunderstanding.

"Well, since the man they're lookin' fer matches your pa's description down to the pistol ball in his laig, I think he may have a hard time convincin' 'em it weren't him. He figured it'd be easier to keep out of their way."

"Papa has a pistol ball in his leg?" I shrieked. "How?"

"I jest told ye; he got shot during a robbery," Job explained impatiently.

"But what was he doing there?"

"The very question the Runners are agoin' to ask him, and I hope he has a better answer than I can give you—he was astealin'."

"Oh Lord," I whispered.

"Save it fer later. Than ye can pray and I'll preach a sermon. Meantimes, meet me out 'ere in the garden at ten tonight." He turned to leave. "And don't tell no one where you're goin'."

CHAPTER TWENTY

Shaken, I returned to the house, climbed the back stairs slowly to my room, and laid down on the canopied bed.

Moments later Eliza bustled into the room. "Are you all right?" she asked anxiously, seeing me staring fixedly upward.

"I have a headache," I lied.

"Do you need anything?" she asked, hovering over me and wringing her hands.

"Just rest. Tell Sarah I won't be down for dinner," I returned faintly.

"I will," she assured me and left with a loud slam of the door.

Alone with my thoughts, I worried. Papa might die before I got to him. Maybe Job hadn't told me the full truth about how bad he was. Why hadn't I asked him more questions, I fretted. By the time ten o'clock crept around I was almost beside myself with fear. Throwing a dark pelisse over my rust-colored day dress, I sneaked down the back stairs through the quiet house and met Job in the garden.

Job led me wordlessly out the back gate and down a great many side streets. As we walked, the neighborhood became increasingly seedy and we passed several boisterous gin houses. Finally Job stopped and knocked twice on a door in an alley. It creaked open and a tall, gaunt woman admitted us after giving us a hard stare. I followed Job inside and up a narrow flight of stairs to a small bedroom with a sloping roof. By the light of two flickering candles I could discern Papa lying on a small bed, his blue eyes open and feverishly bright.

"Bout time ye got here, you rascal," he snapped. "Ye took your own sweet time, didn't ye?"

Job was about to respond in kind when I intervened. "Papa, it's me, Vicky Ann. Are you hurt?"

"Oh, ye here, air ye? Good, good, always glad to see you, Vicky Ann." He raised his head slightly to look at me.

"Papa, I came because Job said you'd been shot," I whispered agitatedly.

"Yes, and damn inconvenient it is too, I kin tell ye. Got the ball out this mornin' though, so I'll be up in a day or two." Then, recalling his attention to me, "What air ye doin' in London? I thought you was with Mrs. Worthy in Kent."

"Worthing, Papa, it's Mrs. Worthing, and I'm staying with some people here. I'm their guest." I stated the last words proudly but Papa quickly put a damper on my pride.

"Yeah? Well watch your purse. Last time I was someone's guest, they robbed me and left my by the side of the road. 'Member that, Job, about five years back? You and me was—"

"Papa, please, tell me what's wrong." I knelt beside his bed and took hold of one feeble hand.

"Wrong? I jest told ye, I caught a ball in my laig. That old heifer downstairs cut it out for me though and I'm fine now." He paused a minute. "I believe I'll go to Gretna Green for a spell. Haven't been to Scotland much lately."

"Papa, what about the Runners?" I thought I would scream from sheer frustration.

"I don't rightly know what about them," he mused. "Seems like they been alookin' for me for a time. Even 'fore I come to town they was lookin' for me. I heerd at the Coxcomb that they were in there two, three weeks ago askin' about me."

"I've had them looking for you," I explained.

His eyes widened in amazement. "Why would you do a thing like that to your own pa, what's always been good to you? Didn't I bring you a nice puppet last year?"

"Papa, I haven't played with puppets for years," I began in exasperation. He looked at me with a hurt expression and I softened my tone. "Papa, you had been gone so long I was worried about you. I thought the Bow Street Runners might be able to find you. How did you get shot anyway?"

"Well, I was avisitin' some people and they was showin' me their gun," Papa began with dignity.

"You see, Vera," Job interjected, "it's like this. Me, Luke Percel, and your Pa was climbin' through the winder of this house, when we hears a shout."

"Shut up, Job!" Papa yelled.

Job continued unabashed. "We looks down to see a man holdin' a gun on us and tellin' us to come down. Luke was already inside the house, I was on the windersill, and your Pa was on the ledge. Luke whips out a gun and shoots the man. The man below shoots his gun jest as he's fallin' and grazes your Pa in the laig. I caught him 'fore he fell and dragged him down the trellis and Luke took off on his own. The man on the ground was in an awful sorry state. I heerd at the Coxcomb that he give a description of your Pa 'fore he died. So they's alookin, fer your Pa for murder," he concluded.

"Oh no," I murmured. I felt very faint.

"And likely they'll git him too unless we can git some money so's we can git out of 'ere."

"Money?" I questioned blankly. "What has that to say to the matter?"

"The wench downstairs is agoin' to turn us both over to the Runners unless we pay for her trouble of housin' us and removin' the ball from your pa's laig. He ain't exactly in no condition to escape out the winder so I reckon we'll have to find some way of payin' her."

"How much money?"

"Twenty pounds," Job replied dejectedly.

"Only twenty pounds?" I asked excitedly. Job and Papa looked at me in surprise. "I have that much in my room!" They exchanged glances of disbelief. "I do," I insisted. "Job, take me back to the house. I'll be right back, Papa." I gave him a hurried kiss before rushing from the room.

We practically ran back to Sarah's house through the dark and winding streets of London. Job waited for me at the back gate of the garden while I hurried down the path to the back door of the house and pulled on it. It was locked. I ran around to the massive front door and pulled hard on it. It, too, was locked. I took hold of the knocker to sound it when the door opened and I was pulled inside still clinging to the knocker. Lord Linton stood squarely in front of me, looking very angry. I moved to dodge around him to the stairs, but he reached a hand out and grasped my arm firmly.

"What are you doing here?" I gasped irrelevantly.

"I don't think that is the major point to be discussed right now," he answered sarcastically. "But to satisfy your lively curiosity, I'll tell you. When you were found missing from your room, I was sent for. I am responsible for you, you know."

"Yes," I agreed breathlessly and tried to move past him.

He held me back. "One minute of your precious time, please."

"Let me by," I pleaded. "I have something very important to do."

"No doubt, Miss Lyons. I find it not at all unusual for someone to plead a headache and retire early and then show up on the doorstep at midnight after a wild night about the town." His voice was chilling, and I dared not look into his face.

"I haven't been out on the town," I answered stiffly.

"No? Where have you been?" he pursued swiftly.

"I'll explain later. I have to meet someone now."

He released me slowly. "I see," he said shortly. "Well, if you have as assignation with a lover, by all means don't let me stop you. And since you've already spent half the night, trysting with him, there's no reason to ruin the rest of the night, is there? From the looks of you, it must have been a night of pure passion." His sarcasm changed to something harsher as he continued,

"But don't come back here. If you intend to live like a slut, then you may operate out of Covent Garden and not Sarah's house."

I looked wearily into his blazing green eyes, opened my mouth to form some reply, and finding none, brushed past him to the stairs. There would be time to explain later, I reassured myself as I scrambled up the steps. Now the most important thing was to get Papa out of London before the Runners found him. I reached my room, grabbed my meager savings from under the dresser scarf, and ran out of the house and back through the garden to Job.

By the time we reached Papa's room again, he had decided twenty pounds was too much and that he could make a better bargain. Over my protests, Papa limped down the stairs and began to harangue with the landlady. To my surprise and Papa's satisfaction, she settled for fifteen pounds and he pocketed the rest of the money. Then he and Job headed slowly out the door. I heard a wagon creak by and knew that they would find a place in it.

I was uncertain what to do next. I looked at the landlady hopefully. She regarded me hostilely. Deciding it would be easier to brave the world outside, I walked out into the street and she slammed the door shut behind me. I started slowly back toward Sarah's house. Lord Linton's words came clearly back to my mind. I knew what he thought of me—what they all must think of me—but I had nowhere else to go.

The streets were deserted and I was not bothered, although I took the precaution of pulling my hood over my head and running past the gin shops. After taking two wrong turns, I arrived at Sarah's house just as the passing Charley announced "two o'clock and all's well." I prayed that he was right and resolutely climbed the steps and banged the knocker.

The door was opened by the imperturbable butler, who evinced no surprise at seeing me. He motioned me to follow him to the study and stood aside for me to enter. Lord Linton was seated at the desk, staring fixedly at the desk top. He looked up from his reverie when the door closed and stood up slowly.

"Where have you been?" he demanded. He had a hard look about him that warned me he would accept nothing but the truth.

"I was with Papa."

His expression changed. There was a look of something like relief on it for a brief moment; then his mouth tightened again. "Your father is here in London? How long have you known this?"

"I didn't know until today. Job came to take me to him. He needed money so I came back for it," I explained nervously.

He regarded me steadily for several minutes, his black hair disheveled and his face taut. He motioned me to a Queen Anne chair, then rose and paced the room, his glare never leaving my face.

Finally I ventured timidly. "I suppose you are angry at me for not telling you the whole of the matter when I came back for the money?"

"An excellent supposition," he bit back sarcastically.

I sunk lower into the chair, wishing fervently to make myself invisible.

"So you felt it necessary to go sneaking around London in the dead of night without ever giving a thought about the concerns of those responsible for you?" Lord Linton interrogated savagely.

The question was phrased rather unfairly, I thought resentfully. It was true that I had thought it necessary to go sneaking around London, but the last part of his sentence distorted my actions. I was saved the necessity of replying when Sarah swept into the room and threw her arms around me.

"Wesley, don't scold the poor child. Can't you see she's white with exhaustion?" She pulled me to my feet and, putting her arm protectively around me, ushered me from the room.

Alone in my room, I tried to sleep, but it eluded me. Rising purposelessly, I descended the stairs, thinking vaguely that I would drink a glass of warm milk to calm my shattered nerves. As I passed the study, I saw a light was still burning. I opened the door noiselessly and looked inside. Lord Linton was sitting gazing into the unlit fireplace. His shoulders sagged and in one hand he grasped a bottle of brandy. He had not heard me enter—indeed his senses seemed dulled to all that was going on around him, and I judged him to be very much the worse for drink. The look on his flushed face was strangely forlorn and weary. I felt an irresistible urge to soothe that look away. Without knowing fully what I intended, I approached him as one mesmerized.

He looked up and smiled a crooked smile. "Ah, the vision from my dreams has materialized," he said in a slurred rush of words. Rising, he stood directly in front of me. I tilted my head back to continue looking into his green jewel eyes and, as if by mutual consent, our lips met and held in a long kiss. I pulled slowly away and the same force that had brought me to the room drew me away.

Back in my room, feeling strangely at peace, I fell into a second sleep. I rose early for breakfast and was surprised to find the marquis sitting alone at the oval table, looking gaunt and weary. He must have passed the night in the study. He wished me a cordial good morning and proceeded to finish his breakfast. His manner indicated nothing of last night. Slowly, regretfully, I realized that he had been drunk enough to have forgotten all about it.

CHAPTER TWENTY-ONE

"Why have you been so dreamy lately?" Maryanne asked.

"Dreamy? Have I been dreamy?" I asked in surprise, looking up from the book I had been pretending to read in the parlor corner of my room.

"Since I have asked that question three times, I would say so."

"I'm sorry. I've just been thinking."

"What's his name?" she demanded with lively curiosity.

"What makes you think it's a man?" I countered. For the past three days I had thought of Lord Linton to the exclusion of all else. I couldn't help myself. His kiss had awakened something in me that I had been trying desperately to suppress.

"It always is a man," Maryanne observed, "that causes women to walk around in a daze. Is he as handsome as Lord Stanton?"

"Maryanne, there are those who do not find that short, beady-eyed man at all attractive."

"Who, for instance?" she asked as she rose from my bed to peer at herself contentedly in the glass. "What of Edward?"

"What of him?"

"Well, you do ride with him every morning in the park. Have you lost your heart to him? Is that why you're mooning about?"

"I like Edward very well," I evaded.

"Do you wish to marry him?"

"Maryanne," I said in exasperation. "I don't wish to discuss the matter any more."

"Well, I think Edward is an excellent choice. Much better than those silly baronets and viscounts who come traipsing up to the house every morning, simpering over you."

"They don't simper!" I denied, although truth to tell, I was beginning to find them just the slightest bit tiresome.

"As I was saying, Edward is far better than they are. It's my belief that you should marry him."

"Thank you for your advice," I returned in a tone that belied my gratitude.

"Oh, I almost forgot to tell you—Lord Linton's *chère amie* has returned to London."

With that alarming bit of news she took her leave, abandoning me to ponder this bitter news alone. I lectured myself severely to put all thought of the marquis from my head. It didn't matter one whit to me if he had a polar bear for a playmate. It was mulberries to mildew that he wasn't going to offer for me, so there was no point fretting about who he did choose to pass his time with. But even after my stern and rational lecture to myself, I still felt dejected.

I became even more dejected when I arrived at Lady Marley's soirée the next evening. Lary Marley's idea of entertaining was in the last-century fashion of grouping chairs in a circle about the salon and seating the guests around the circle to exchange self-conscious commonplaces. The fact that there must have been eighty chairs circling the large salon did not make for a more cozy or intimate group. Mercifully someone at last began to play a tune on the pianoforte and brought a little relief to the strained assembly.

In the midst of the song Lord Linton appeared in the doorway with a blond-haired woman on his arm. It was the first time I had ever seen him anywhere with a woman and my heart lurched. I must confess they made a striking couple—my tall, arrogantly handsome, dark-haired guardian and this beauty with sculpted features and hazel, almond-shaped eyes set bewitchingly against her satin skin.

She was so lovely that I stared at her unabashedly as she and her escort seated themselves. "Who is she?" I finally managed to ask Maryanne.

Maryanne wrenched her attention away from the corner of the room Lord Stanton was gracing. "Who?"

"The girl with Lord Linton." I affected casualness.

"That's Lady Clarissa. She's been gone for several weeks. I think she was visiting a sister in Bath. It's not at all like her to miss so many social events, but it's my belief she's playing a little game of strategy. Her husband has been dead a trifle less than a year. Lady Clare hopes to entice Lord Linton to marry her, but so far he hasn't come up to scratch. She left town for a time, under the dubious delusion that her presence would be missed, but I see she has returned opportunely near the one-year anniversary of her husband's death. Now she's free to accept Wesley."

"Silence, everyone," Lady Marley clapped her

hands and demanded from the center of the room. "Mrs. Uston has volunteered to play a few pieces on the pianoforte so that our dear young people may have an opportunity to stand up and dance just a little. I don't usually do this, but I thought tonight—"

Her last words were drowned in the noise of chairs scraping on the parquet floor as the entire assembly stood and began to mill about, the men seeking partners and the women seeking to make themselves available.

My first partner was a frosty Lord Mitford. I hadn't spoken with him since our parting at the Bridgewater's ball. His sole purpose in soliciting a dance with me seemed to be to give himself a chance to relate his scorn for chits who throw themselves at a man's head but are unwilling to express their emotions in more physical terms.

"I didn't throw myself at your head," I objected. "I didn't throw anything at all. I did kick you but that's not precisely the same thing as throwing—"

"Do be silent," he hissed. "Do you want everyone here to know that we're quarreling?"

"You started it," I bristled.

He murmured a pithy expletive into my shocked ear before declaring that the next chit of my ilk who set her cap for him would be sent about her business very shortly, even if she was the daughter of a Russian prince.

The conclusion of the dance prevented me the satisfaction of informing him I had never set my cap for him.

My next partner was the aging but young-at-heart Sir Amberton. As I moved about the room with him, my eyes alighted on Lord Linton. He was seated cozily in a corner of the room having a *tête-à-tête* with the devastating Clarissa. I looked hastily away as she gave him a seductively coy smile and engaged my surprised partner in frenziedly bright talk.

Edward claimed me next. "I am indeed lucky tonight," he said. "Not only have I been able to treat myself to several glimpses of Lady Forest's hair—it's a curious shade of purple tonight, I fear she'll have to wear a hat or dye it again—but I also have the rare privilege of standing up with you." He watched me curiously. "Something seems to be the matter here. What's amiss?"

"Oh nothing," I replied lightly, not wanting Edward to suspect that the sight of Lord Linton with Clarissa had upset me terribly.

"Hmmm. Let's see. Could you be jealous because Lord Stanton is paying marked attention to Maryanne? You haven't set your cap for him, have you? Several girls are already wearing the willow for him and I fear Maryanne will fare no better."

I shook my head. "I haven't set my cap for Lord Stanton."

He glanced around the room at the passing couples. "I don't see anyone else who could be having such an effect on you. I don't think it's Lord Mitford, since he has looked quite Friday-faced following his dance with you. Is it that young swain over there in the purple unmentionables that's set your heart aflutter?"

"They're brown," I retorted.

"A true love, in whatever colored trousers, is a true love," he reasoned.

I smiled. "You're fair and far out in your guesses, sir."

"Then perhaps it's me you're pining away for."

I was about to respond tartly when the expression on his face stopped me. He was looking seriously down into my face and I looked back into his honest face uncertainly. The dance ended, and he led me off the floor, bowed, and left me with Sarah. I gazed dumbly after him.

"You look as if you're in a trance, dear," Sarah's voice broke into my thoughts. "And Mr. Genson here is complimenting you very prettily on your amber chiffon gown and asking for a dance."

I walked out onto the floor with Mr. Genson, my mind working to understand the events of the evening. Did Edward mean to imply that he had a *tendre* for me? Maryanne had said that he had been married before, and I didn't think I could compare very favorably with a childhood sweetheart, especially one who had been well-bred.

Then there was the marquis. He was tall, dark, and handsome and I knew I could never hope to attract him. The presence of Clarissa on his arm tonight had been proof of that. He might engage in a light flirtation with me but never anything serious. That knowledge caused a curious fluttering in my throat.

"Most charming with its lacy flounces and delicate little train." Mr. Genson was still extolling the virtues of my gown as he led me back to Sarah.

She was sitting in a corner with Maryanne. Maryanne was wistfully watching Lord Stanton about the room as I sat down beside her.

"Isn't he handsome?" Maryanne sighed.

"Who?" I feigned ignorance.

"Lord Stanton. He's so attractive with his pearly teeth and dark eyes. And he's an elegant small size; not like some of these gangling oafs."

"You don't speak from any particular interest, do you, Maryanne?" Sarah teased.

"I know you think I see him as being more than he is, but that's not true. If you could know him as I know him, you'd understand he's not a gazetted fortune hunter. He's a poet."

"If Sarah could know him as you know him, I think her poor dead husband would be turning over in his grave," Edward offered as he joined us. "I have seen you leave the room with that weasel several times. I can't understand how a cur like that without a penny to bless himself with can continue to attract the attenion of respectable girls."

Maryanne drew herself up haughtily. "I don't like it above half that you are casting aspersions on Lord Stanton's character."

"What character?" Edward inquired interestedly.

"Maryanne, you didn't leave the house with him? It's most improper and people will have altogether the wrong impression of you," Sarah said worriedly.

"We only stepped outside the door once or twice when the heat in the room became too stifling."

"Maryanne," Sarah began severely, "you are not to indulge in a flirtation with that rake. He has been the cause of more than one family disgrace."

"You don't know him as I do," Maryanne pouted.

Edward cleared his throat to warn of an approacher.

209

Maryanne and Sarah automatically composed their faces into smiles and looked up to greet the newcomer, all unpleasant talk suspended for the moment.

Sarah's smile froze and Maryanne's widened to genuineness as she beheld her maligned suitor. "Eric, er, Lord Stanton, we were just speaking of you."

"Indeed," he smiled, revealing a row of pearly, if crooked, teeth. "Nothing bad, I trust."

"Oh no," Maryanne cooed.

"Good evening, Lord Stanton," Sarah greeted him in quelling tones.

He smiled at her and Edward before turning to me. "Since I've already danced with Maryanne twice, I came to request the honor of little Miss Lyons for the next dance."

I forced a smile and allowed him to lead the way to the dance floor. "They don't approve of me, you know." He opened the conversation by going directly to the point.

At a loss for words I concentrated on my steps.

"Did you hear me?"

"Uh, yes, yes I did," I faltered.

"But you have no cause to suspect me of any misdeeds, have you?"

"I don't know," I answered truthfully, looking up into his calculating face.

He laughed, a rather forced, unpleasant sound. "Well, at any rate you certainly can't object to doing me one small favor."

"What is it?" I asked suspiciously.

"Dear me, you are enchanting when your little black brows furrow together and those incredible blue eyes darken in distrust."

210

"What is it?" I demanded louder.

"Hush! Do you want the whole room to hear you?" he hissed. "I merely wished you to convey this missive to Maryanne."

"Why don't you give it to her?"

"My dear simpleminded child," he explained patiently. "Wipe that mulish expression off your face and listen to me. I have to leave immediately, and there was little way I could snatch Maryanne from the bosom of her scowling family even long enough to deliver a note."

"Why don't you have it sent round to the house tomorrow?" I argued.

"Because it might be intercepted. Now, will you give it to her like a good little girl?" he wheedled.

"No."

"Come now, I can't be such a ramshackle fellow as your hurtful words would imply. After all—Maryanne likes me."

"Well," I hesitated.

"I assure you on my word as a gentleman that there is nothing improper in it," he urged.

"All right," I agreed finally. "But I shall not do it again," I stated emphatically to show him what a hard person I was to deal with.

"Of course not," he returned silkily. "Well, I must be off."

"But the dance isn't over," I said in confusion as he slipped the note into the wide white ribbon below my chest.

"It is for us," he replied as he led me through the dancing couples back to Sarah and dumped me unceremoniously.

211

CHAPTER TWENTY-TWO

The next evening found us on our way to another social function. The Season was in full swing, and Sarah didn't want us to miss any of the events. I was wearing my new yellow silk gown with silver piping about the scooped neck and around the tiny puff sleeves. My hair was caught on top of my head in a little topknot, and yellow primroses formed a halo around it. I was wearing new yellow slippers, and I could hardly wait to dance.

We arrived at Mrs. Waite's rout a little early. The aging butler ushered us into a small drawing room that was full of card tables. I counted rapidly. There were six tables and no refreshments in sight. Mrs. Waite, it turned out, had one predilection and one predilection only—and it was cards. The tables were already half filled with avid cardplayers.

"This is the beginner's room," Sarah whispered. "If you win enough games in here, she moves you on to the dining room where the better players are. If you win there, she moves you to the blue salon where the best players are."

"Oh," I said doubtfully. My card-playing experience with Papa had taught me how to cheat skillfully, but unless I cheated, I rarely won a game. I didn't think this was the place to exercise my expertise as a card cheat. It would be most embarrassing if I were caught.

"Where is Mrs. Waite?" I whispered.

"In the blue salon, but she'll come through in a short while. Maryanne and I will be in the dining room and Edward will be in the blue salon when he arrives." At my forsaken look she reassured me, "You won't be left alone. There's Andrea Hogg-Devine; you know her."

I settled myself resignedly beside the fat, dull-witted Andrea. I fast learned that the poor girl was nearly as bad a cardplayer as I. In fact I don't believe she could have won even if she had been allowed to cheat. Fortunately her partner was able to win in spite of her.

The room was soon full but, except for quick intakes of breath over a particularly good or a particularly bad card, it was depressingly silent. I tried once to make small talk, but I met with such fierce frowns from the wizened dowager beside me that I quickly desisted.

I played several games of cards before the boredom of losing constantly began to annoy me. I feared I would resort to cheating if I stayed much longer. The entrance of a newcomer gave me my means of escape.

"Excuse me," I murmured, "would you mind if that gentleman who just entered took my place? I need a breath of air."

Andrea and the dowager met my leave-taking with indifference; my disgruntled partner met it with undisguised joy.

Escaping from the room, I wandered down the hall

214

and out the open French doors that led to the garden. Guided by the soft moonlight and the glow from the house, I followed the flagstones through the garden, past neatly clipped hedges, and winded around on the path until I came to a small marble pond.

The water surface was partially covered with water lilies, and I could see white and red flowers floating on the pads. Peering closer, I saw swimming goldfish and near me, very near, was a perfectly motionless fish, its mouth circled into an "O" right at the surface of the water. I bent very quietly and then, with a flurry of fingers, swooped to grab it. The fish eluded me, and I fell very gracelessly into the water, landing on my hands with a painful scrape. I stood up slowly in the shallow, rippling water, rubbing the palms of my sore hands against my dripping gown.

"What in God's name is going on?"

I looked reluctantly up into the shadowed face of Lord Wesley Linton. There was no need to see his face to know his feelings. His anger had been borne through on every biting syllable.

It wanted only this, I thought ruefully as I took a deep breath and gave my limp explanation. "I was trying to catch a goldfish."

He swore under his breath and reached in a sinewy arm to haul me out of the water. "You don't need a husband, you need a nursemaid," he snarled.

I said nothing. I felt humiliated, cold, and uncomfortable. My chin was trembling, but I was determined not to cry.

"At least you're not crying," he said harshly as he took his caped coat off and wrapped it around me.

"Let's get out of here. No, not that way; you can't go back into the house looking like that. I'll take you home." He led me through the garden and out into a courtyard. He ordered a startled groom to bring his carriage, and I was shortly seated across from him on the way back to Sarah's house.

"Are you hurt?" he asked indifferently after a few moments.

My humiliation had given way to bad temper. "Hurt? No, I quite enjoyed it. It refreshed me to feel the scrape of my hands on rock and to feel my wringing wet dress clinging to me in the cool of the night air."

"It serves you right," he snapped. Then in a softer, more sensual tone he continued, "And your dress clings charmingly."

I gasped and turned my head quickly to the window.

"Another thing," Lord Linton continued, apparently deciding that, since I was a captive audience, he would take the opportunity to rid himself of all the barbs he had been saving. "I've seen the way you smirk and simper around Edward and I want you to know that dangling after him won't serve."

I maintained a stony silence.

" 'Why won't it?' you say?" The marquis readily supplied my end of the conversation. "I'll tell you since you are so mightily interested. It won't serve because he has already been through one disastrous marriage and he's not looking to get leg-shackled again.

"Maryanne said he was happily married," I countered sulkily.

"Well, he wasn't," Lord Linton retorted. "Seeing his marriage soured me on the holy state almost as much as it did him."

"Is that why you're not married?" I asked in fascination.

"No, I am not married because—" He stopped. "What am I doing discussing this with you?" he asked himself in a harried tone. "We're here, mermaid," he announced as we rolled up in front of Sarah's house.

He escorted me inside and watched from the foyer as I mounted the stairs with all the dignity I could muster in a sopping gown with shoes that squished on the carpet. I tromped into my room and explained to a wide-eyed Eliza that I had been caught in a torrential downpour.

"It didn't rain here," she informed me in awestruck tones as she helped me out of my yellow silk gown. "Isn't it odd that it should rain in a part of town not five blocks from here and not rain here?" Her simple face mirrored her surprise at this unusual occurrence.

"Yes, it is. If you'll excuse me, Eliza, I'd like to go to sleep now."

She blew out the candles and took the last one out with her. But what seemed like only five minutes later the room was fully lit again.

"Are you asleep?" Maryanne inquired, shaking me as she asked the question.

I sat up groggily in bed. "I was asleep until you woke me," I answered as fiercely as I could manage in my sleep-laden state.

"I wondered if you had any more notes from Eric."

"I thought his name was Lord Stanton," I said

crisply, "and I certainly do not have any more notes from him. I should be committed to Bedlam for giving you the first one."

"Oh it wasn't the first one," Maryanne confided. "I've had several."

"I shall tell Sarah that he writes to you," I bluffed.

Maryanne was nonplussed. "You wouldn't do that, would you? You know she disapproves of him. She thinks he has an impoverished title and he's hanging out for a fortune. Actually he doesn't need money at all."

"How do you know?"

"Because he told me," she replied simply.

"That's doing it a bit brown, Maryanne. The man is probably lying."

"Never!" she cried, rising from the bed and pacing angrily to the door. She closed it with a resounding bang.

I tried to lull myself back to sleep, but my guilt kept me from it. I should have never given her Lord Stanton's note, I lamented. I should have torn it up and thrown the pieces away. And since I'd been widgeon enough to give her the note, I should make things right by telling Sarah. That was exactly what I should do.

But the next day I not only didn't tell Sarah, I managed to involve myself deeper in Maryanne's romance. It happened while Maryanne and I were in the billiard room watching Edward and the marquis play a game. I had eschewed the game for fear I would win a camel or something even harder to ride than a horse. As I observed their game, I saw Maryanne about to slyly pass a note to a footman. At that precise moment

Sarah entered the room and Maryanne looked quickly around for a place to hide her letter. In a loyal effort to help Maryanne, I engaged Sarah's attention. After two more successful games Lord Linton picked up his coat and left.

Sarah and Edward drifted out to the other room. I turned to Maryanne. Her face was a study in bewilderment.

"What's amiss?" I asked.

"Wesley just left with my letter," she wailed.

"How could he do that?"

"I put it in his coat when Sarah came in and I didn't have a chance to take it out before he left." Tears welled up in her eyes. "What am I going to do? When he reads that letter, he's sure to give it to Sarah."

"It can't be as bad as all that," I soothed. "You and Sarah are always at dagger's drawing anyway."

"This is different. I'm afraid I've said some terribly indiscreet things."

"Like what?" I asked interestedly.

"I can't tell you," she moaned, "but if word of this gets out, it would ruin me, and no one would ever offer for me."

"Don't be a goose. Lord Linton would never show it to anyone but Sarah or Edward."

Maryanne brightened at this thought, but her face immediately fell. "I'm not sure that's not the worst part of all—having Sarah see what I've written." She looked mournfully at the floor for a moment, then raised her head defiantly. "We'll just have to get it back, that's all."

"Whatever are you talking about? Lord Linton is already home by now."

"Right, but I doubt that he'll stay. He'll go home to change clothes and then pass the night with some doxy somewhere. We have only to go to his house and remove the note from his coat."

I looked at her in astonishment. "You can't be serious! You don't go to a gentleman's house alone."

"Oh, yes we can," she replied firmly.

The entrance of a footman forced us to adjourn to Maryanne's bedroom. Once there, she turned to me with an odd look on her face. "Oh dear," she breathed softly, "when Wes finds that note, he won't know that it isn't for him."

"Why not?"

"Because it begins: 'My love.' "

The full impact of her words hit me. Lord Linton was to be the recipient of one of Maryanne's girlish, impassioned love notes and think it was meant for him. I made a careful study of the silver threads interwoven in the mint-green drapes so that she wouldn't see the laughter I was fighting to suppress. After a moment I had mastered myself enough to ask, "If you didn't address it to Lord Stanton, did you sign your name?"

She nodded regretfully, "That's the rub. I signed it, 'Until I see you at midnight in the garden, I am your Melancholy Maryanne.' "

"You were trysting with him in the garden?" I asked, shocked.

"Tonight was the first time," she said defensively.

"Oh."

"Well," she said resolutely, "there's nothing for it but to go to his house."

"You simply cannot go to his house." I felt it my duty to interject a little sense into the discussion.

She regarded me speculatively. "Not me, we."

I shook my head firmly. Maryanne wheedled, cajoled, and attempted to bribe me. I stood firm. My resolution broke only when her large brown eyes filled with tears and her voice broke on a sobbing note. I was ever a soft touch, I thought wearily. "All right, I'll go with you."

The plan was simple, and—Maryanne assured me—completely foolproof. We would wear some of Edward's old clothes, go to Lord Linton's house, retrieve the note, and return.

Half an hour later, well past midnight, we crept downstairs and stole out the side door. I felt utterly ridiculous with my hair bunched up under a beaver hat that was pulled down to my eyebrows, my shoulders hunched up to give height to Edward's last year's riding coat, and my feet clomping in shoes so large there was a pair of stockings stuffed in each toe. I hiked up my breeches and muttered my discontent as we walked rapidly down the street to the marquis's house.

"I scarcely think it matters what you are wearing," Maryanne returned. "This is not to be a social function where your clothes will be scrutinized."

"A lucky thing too because I am about to lose my trousers."

"Quiet," she ordered. "We're here."

I looked up at the large dark house before me apprehensively. It was larger and even more grand looking than Sarah's with its pedimented door and high, arched windows. Maryanne took my hand and led me around the back of the house to the garden. Amazingly the back door was open. We exchanged glances of surprise in the pale moonlight before Maryanne pulled me through it and dragged me up the stairs behind her.

We stopped at the landing on the second floor. I looked nervously around. The hall was very dimly lit by a candle burning at the other end. "Which do you think is his room?" I whispered.

"We'll just have to try all of the doors; he has no guests, so he should be the only person with a room on this floor. The servants sleep on the third floor."

We tiptoed over and opened the first door. The curtains were open and we could discern that the room was unoccupied. Closing the door as carefully as possible, I followed Maryanne down the hall. We were rewarded on our fourth try. We entered a sitting room where we could distinguish a man's beaver hat thrown carelessly on a chair. Maryanne closed the door and lit a candle. I looked cautiously around the rich red and gold room.

"His bedroom is behind that door," she said, jerking her head toward a heavy door.

"Ssssh, do you want someone to hear you?" I whispered. "He may even be in there if his hat is here."

Having come this far, Maryanne was dauntless. "I tell you he's off sleeping with some fancy piece somewhere."

"What if his valet is here?"

"Don't be silly. All valets go downstairs to chase the maids around when their masters are gone." She grabbed my arm and propelled me over to the bedroom door, pushed the door open, and ventured inside. The window curtains were drawn shut, making the huge room very dark even with the light from our flickering candle. The bed curtains were also closed. I stood rigidly by the door as Maryanne searched for several seconds. Finally she exclaimed softly, "I've got it."

We hastened back out the door, down the steps, and out through the garden. We slipped back into Sarah's house undetected.

CHAPTER TWENTY-THREE

I did not see Lord Linton for the next several days. I was still rankling from his talk with me in the carriage when he had told me I was making a cake of myself over Edward. Now I was uncomfortable with Edward when we went out for our morning rides or sat together in the evenings after dinner. I tried to be very sedate so that he wouldn't think I was throwing myself at him but, in an effort to return me to my old self, he usually said something so outrageously funny that I couldn't contain my laughter.

On the other front I was still praying for a miracle that would send Lord Linton into my arms. Pictures of his handsome countenance and appealing green eyes sprang unbidden into my mind at frequent intervals. I tried to banish them with stern little talks to myself, but they were rebellious little thoughts and kept cropping up in spite of my best efforts to subdue them. I knew if Lord Linton thought that I was a silly chit when he mistakenly accused me of trying to attract Edward, he would go off into whoops of laughter at the idea that I really wanted to attract him.

Poor Maryanne was having her love problems too. Her elation over recovering her note was marred by the fact that she did not see nor hear from Lord Stanton during the following week.

At the end of the week I saw Lord Linton at a small party given by an eccentric and tone-deaf dowager. The evening's entertainment was the solo performance of an Italian singer. After the tenor warbled to a close, the guests were ushered to a tiny room crowded with bright green overstuffed chairs for refreshments. The guests were predominantly older men and women anxious to prose on about the singer's voice. I escaped down the hall to the empty library to curl up in a wing chair and munch my stale piece of cake in peace.

"Lovely evening, is it not?" a drawling voice asked.

I looked up warily to see Lord Linton framed in the doorway. "It is," I agreed.

"Nearly as lovely as last week but lacking the full moon," he continued as he closed the door and stood watching me.

I stared at him in confusion.

"Come now, Miss Lyons, let's be honest with each other. Is there anything particular you wish to tell me about last week?" he inquired pleasantly.

I looked guiltily around for a diversion. Finding none, I decided to brazen it out. "Then you know about our trip to the house?"

"Yes," he responded silkily, crossing the room to lean his elbow negligently on the wooden mantelpiece.

"How?" I asked bluntly.

"Upon finding the note in my pocket, I knew that Maryanne would not be far behind, which is why I conveniently left my house door open. I must confess that I was not unduly shocked to see you with her."

"I thought we were so quiet," I mused.

"You have all the stealthiness of an army on the march. If I had not known you were coming, I would most assuredly have been awakened by you."

"Oh dear." I made a careful study of the carved walnut mantelpiece beside his lordship.

"In fact," he continued in a pleasant tone, "I personally escorted you home to make certain you came to no harm."

"Oh dear," I repeated worriedly and shifted my eyes from the mantel to the floor before asking in barely audible words. "What are you going to do?"

"Do? I've already done it," he returned jovially.

"What did you do?" I asked, daring to gaze into his amused face.

"First of all," he confided, "I knew the instant I saw the note that it was not written for me."

"How did you know that? It didn't have a name on it."

"True. However, I flatter myself I don't arouse such cheap sentiments in young girls' breasts. It was such a simpering letter that I surmised it was meant for some young dandy. Having seen the way Maryanne moons after Lord Stanton, I decided he fit handily into my picture of the sop who inspired the note. I took the liberty of calling on him and had a short talk with him. He was able to see the advisability of going back to his financially beleaguered estate for an extended visit."

"How strange. Maryanne says he much prefers London to the country. How did you persuade him to leave?"

Lord Linton extended a long hand to carefully inspect his fingernails before replying. "I relied heavily on tact and charm and only made the merest reference to physical violence if he chose to stay. As it turned out, he had been meaning to remove back to his estate anyway. So he left. Now that he is disposed of, there's one less person I have to deal with over the matter."

"What are you going to do to us?" I scarcely dared ask.

"I'm going to have a brief talk with Melancholy. I think that's all that will be required. If she doesn't see things my way immediately, I believe I can bring her around."

I had not the slightest doubt that he could. Puzzlingly he made no further mention to my part in the escapade. I accepted with alacrity his offer to escort me back to the party. I found myself suddenly eager to prose about the tenor with aging guests.

Just what the marquis said to Maryanne, she did not discuss with me. However, she was much chastened the following day. She was going through a dismal catalog of people "who would be sorry when she was gone"—Lord Linton's name was coming up quite frequently—when I was summoned downstairs for a meeting with the man himself. I found him in the garden standing before a cone-shaped evergreen.

I glanced quickly down at my mauve muslin dress with its wilting little bows about the high bodice. If I had known he was coming, I would have put on my dashing new plum dress that was tight about the hips and had flounces from the knee down to the ground. I would have appeared to much better advantage in that.

"Where is your father?" Lord Linton began without any preliminary pleasantries. Apparently he didn't care what I was wearing.

"I don't know."

"Where did he say he was going when he left London?"

"He didn't."

Lord Linton favored me with a withering look. "You don't seem to be a fountain of information this morning."

"I'm sorry. Papa just didn't confide in me. Truth to tell, I don't think he knew where he was going, although he did mention Gretna Green. But that was weeks ago, and it wouldn't be at all like Papa to stay in one place long."

"Well, I have obtained some information that puts quite a new light on his situation. Luke Percel was shot last night breaking into a store. He died just after the authorities arrived, but it seems he made some sort of deathbed confession about being the one who killed the man who shot your father. That means your father is no longer being pursued by the Runners and is free to come back to England if he has left the country."

"Papa has been proven innocent?" I asked excitedly.

"I wouldn't go that far," the marquis answered dryly. "However, he has been cleared of the charge of murder."

"That's wonderful!" I shouted.

"Yes, it is," he agreed sedately. "Now, if we only had some way to let him know."

My face fell. "I really don't know. It doesn't seem very likely that he would contact the woman who

229

fixed up his leg. They weren't best friends," I explained. "Wait. He did mention the name of the place where he had heard the Runners were looking for him. They might know how to get in touch with him there."

"What was the name?"

"Let's see, it started with a 'C.' Chicken? No. Cabbage? No. Cantalope?" I bit my lower lip in concentration.

"Was he describing his favorite food or the place where he had heard about the warrant?" Lord Linton's voice held a trace of humor.

"I've got it," I cried. "Coxcomb, the Coxcomb."

"The Coxcomb," he repeated the words slowly.

"Have you heard of it?" I asked in surprise.

"No, but then I rather expect it's not my usual sort of place," he replied dryly. "Never fear, I'll find out where it is and go there this afternoon to try and discover what they can tell me about your father."

I clutched his sleeve as he turned to leave. "No, I had better go," I said anxiously.

He regarded me skeptically. "I don't think it is going to be the place for a young lady."

"But if they see you looking as you do now, they'll think it's a trick to bring Papa into public," I protested.

He gazed ruefully from his immaculate, well-cut blue coat and impeccable gray breeches down to his polished black boots. "It's no matter," he shrugged. "I can change my appearance."

Still clutching at his sleeve, I argued, "Yes, but you cannot change that indefinable air of quality about you."

He looked at me with surprise in his green eyes. "Do I have such an air?"

I nodded. "I'm very much afraid you do, and the bartender would suspect you the minute you entered his establishment." I let go of his coat, leaving a damp, wrinkled spot, and stepped back.

"Tell me, is it an annoying air?"

"Oh no! I like it." I stopped in confusion. I had not meant to so boldly state my feelings.

He regarded me somberly. "Thank you," he said quietly. "I shall call for you this afternoon, and we shall both go to the Coxcomb. Can you be ready at two o'clock?"

I nodded and he bowed and left.

He arrived back at the house precisely at two. I scampered out to the carriage before he had a chance to come to the door. I was wearing an apple green dress with white satin trim around the long sleeves and fichu collar. It was hardly appropriate attire for the gin shop I suspected we were heading for, but then, I reasoned, it was appropriate attire for riding in the marquis's carriage.

"I assume that you did not tell Sarah where you are going?"

"No, I didn't think it wise," I confessed as I retied my stylish white bonnet.

"Good, she'd have my head if she knew the part of town I'm taking you to—unchaperoned, to boot." He settled back against the squabs.

We left the widely spaced houses and well-kept buildings gradually behind and ventured into a more seedy section of London. Once or twice the groom stopped the carriage to ask directions of passersby. I giggled as they looked askance at our carriage; this was hardly the sort of vehicle that must normally frequent the establishment.

My suspicion was confirmed when we pulled up before a decaying wooden building where several disheveled patrons were lying about the doorway adorning the sidewalk in front of the shop. Lord Linton took my arm and we stepped past them. The interior was everything I had imagined and less. The half-full room was crowded with tables, many of them supporting men who had passed out over their last drink. Bawds were scattered about at other tables, singing morose songs to themselves or telling ribald jokes to their cronies. The smoke was so heavy there was a blue haze in the room.

The marquis steered me through to a burly man in the back wearing a grimy white apron. His lordship had a few private words with the man, gave him some money, spoke again in a low voice, and more money passed hands. The bartender was shaking his head stubbornly. He had never heard of Robert Lyons, he insisted.

"Please," I blurted out, "Papa must have been known here. This is where he found out the Runners were looking for him."

Several people, who had been regarding us with sidelong glances, looked up, openly curious at this last bit of knowledge.

The barkeeper looked at me in amazement. "You don't look like the type of person who would be a daughter to the type of man who would come here, if you see what I mean and if you don't mind my saying so, begging your pardon, ma'am."

"Robert Lyons is my father," I maintained stoutly. "And if you know where he is, you should tell me." The barkeeper looked doubtful. I pressed my advantage. "I can describe him, that will prove I know him."

"Well, there's a lot of people who might could describe this Robert Lyons you say you're looking for, but that wouldn't necessisarily make that person this other person's daughter, if you get my meaning."

"But I am his daughter," I insisted. "Why would I be here looking for him otherwise?"

"There's other people that might be looking for this Robert Lyons that you say you're looking for, such as the Bow Street Runners, which you yourself just mentioned and I didn't know anything about until you did mention it just a minute ago, if you understand what I'm trying to say."

"Tell her," a man behind me advised the bartender.

The shopkeeper looked past me to my champion. "And supposing I was to know, which I'm not saying that I do, why would I tell her when she may or may not be who she says she is, which is the daughter of this Robert Lyons that she's looking for and that I never heard of before today, answer me that?"

"Tell her because she is who she says she is." I turned to regard the man who had come to my defense. There was something vaguely familiar about him, but I couldn't call to mind where I had met him. He smiled graciously and inclined his head. "I see you remember me from our wonderful night together on the pastoral English countryside? I must confess that I hardly recognized you, but I did recognize your melodious voice."

"Yes," I replied agitatedly, "do you know where my father is?"

"Alas, I fear I do not. However, my brother, who has the misfortune of being both overly verbose and the proprietor of this establishment, can tell you. If he doesn't shortly deliver that information, I shall have to resort to stronger means of making my request. In fact, it appears that your associate is about to take just such stronger measures himself."

I turned to Lord Linton, who did indeed look a thundercloud. He was clenching and unclenching his fists at his side. I could tell it was with all the patience he could muster that he restrained himself from hitting both of the blathering brothers.

The bartender resumed, "I fear I cannot give you directions." Lord Linton took a menacing step forward. "However," he added hastily, "I offer this solution, which appears to me to be a fair solution and that is that if you will leave your direction, I shall have this Robert Lyons, whom I do now remember having had the pleasure of meeting, come to that direction if he does know you and if he does choose to come, which is not to say that he will, but he might, if you understand the gist of that."

"That is the only thing you have said so far that I understand the gist of," the marquis snarled. He left brief instructions to Sarah's residence and took my arm to guide me out to the carriage.

Once inside the carriage he glowered at me. "Well?" he demanded gruffly.

The excitement of having found some fragile link to Papa had brought color to my cheeks and put a sparkle in my eyes. "Isn't it wonderful?" I enthused.

234

"Who was that man in there that you knew?" The words were bitten out.

"I don't know his name," I answered in surprise.

"You spent a wonderful night together in the English countryside and you don't even know his name?" He sounded incredulous.

"I didn't!" I was appalled by the meaning of his words. "I mean, I did talk to him late one night, well early one morning, but that was all."

"Victoria, you are beginning to sound like those two idiots in there both talking at once. Now, as concisely as possible, tell me how it is that you know him."

"He was at Stonehenge and he was up early one morning when I was up. We talked for a while and that was all."

"What did you talk about?" he demanded harshly.

"Stonehenge," I replied truthfully.

The tautness of his cheek muscles relaxed slightly as I stared at him solemnly. "I'm sorry, pet. I know that you weren't involved with him the way he made it sound. God, I should have called him out for insinuating such things in front of all those people."

I giggled. "I don't think it very likely that the word will get about, since I don't recall ever seeing any of those people at the balls I have attended."

His mouth curved into a lopsided grin. "You're right. All the same, that man had better learn to guard his tongue."

"Is that what made you lose your temper?" I asked in awe.

"Yes," he answered shortly.

I digested this information slowly. Lord Linton had been angry at the insinuation that I was a loose woman. Not four months earlier he had been willing to make me a loose woman. What had happened? Was he so reformed that he now upheld virtue and struck down those who did not? Or was it something else? As much as I speculated in my mind how Lord Linton might feel about me, I could come to no clear decision.

CHAPTER TWENTY-FOUR

The following morning Lord Linton joined Edward and me for a ride in the park. It was a wonderful time to be in Hyde Park, before the crowds that followed later in the day. The birds sang cheerily and the stillness of the green was largely unbroken by all but the sounds of nature. That was why we all looked with interest at the lone rider who approached us. As the horse neared, I could see that it was a woman.

"La," a dainty voice said as the visitor reined her horse in by ours, "fancy meeting you here, Wesley." She inclined her head prettily to Edward. "Good morning, Edward." Then, with an engaging smile, she turned her attention to me. "And who have we here?"

"Good morning, Clarissa. Lady Clarissa Seymour, this is Victoria Lyons. Victoria is a guest in our house," Edward said.

As Edward made the introductions, I noted with dismay that Lady Clarissa was even lovelier up close than she had been from a distance. Her skin was alabaster with delicate pink spots in each cheek. Her hazel eyes twinkled, and her smile revealed even, little teeth behind full red lips. Her blonde hair escaped enchantingly from her brown velvet hat set jauntily to one side of her head and secured with a brown satin ribbon beneath her chin. She was wearing a brown velvet riding habit, and she graced her sidesaddle as if she were born to it. I shifted uncomfortably on my own mare.

Lady Clarissa extended a delicate, gloved hand to me. "I'm very pleased to meet you. I've heard ever so much about you. They say your father was a Russian prince. What is it like in Russia?"

"The buildings all have onion-shaped tops, very like the Royal Pavilion at Brighton," Edward supplied. "Is that not so, Victoria?"

"Y-yes," I stammered, "very like the Pavilion." Never having seen either, I didn't think it was a lie to compare them.

"But what brings you to the park at this hour of the morning, Clarissa?" Lord Linton interposed. "I must confess I didn't know you were an early riser."

"Wesley," her words were provocative, "I have of late acquired a great many habits that you may not be aware of. It has been some time since you have called on me, you know." She tapped his arm with one long, gloved finger in a playfully reproving gesture.

"Why don't you join us for a ride, Clarissa?" Edward suggested. "The horses are getting restless."

"I wouldn't want to intrude," she replied sweetly.

The gentlemen assured her that she would not be intruding and, as I watched, she and Lord Linton cantered off together down the road, leaving Edward and me to plod along behind. We rode along for several minutes in silence before I realized that Edward was watching me intently.

"Why are you staring at me?" I asked haughtily.

"I want to see how you are taking the rivalry," he said with lazy humor.

"She's not my rival," I declared defensively. "She just happened to come to the park this morning and ended up riding with us."

Edward tossed his reddish curls back and gave a hoot of laughter. "My dear, Clarissa does not just 'happen' to do anything. She is here this morning because we are here."

"She is?" I puzzled over this information. "How did she know that we would be here?"

"Clarissa makes it her business to know the comings and goings of the man she intends to marry. If she finds that he is taking another young lady to the park, she feels compelled to remedy the situation."

"Oh, then it's quite decided that she and Lord Linton are going to be married?"

"As far as she is concerned, yes."

I bent my head to the horse. The news left me more than a little forlorn. It wasn't, of course, that I had any aspirations of marrying Lord Linton. Still the news that he might marry someone else had a strangely upsetting effect on me. I straightened determinedly. I certainly wasn't going to let anyone think I cared a pin whether Lord Linton married Clarissa or not. I engaged Edward in bright and meaningless chatter during the remainder of the ride.

But while I might be able to lie to all the world, I could not lie to myself. The overwhelming truth was that I did care if Lord Linton married Clarissa. I cared if he even smiled at her. I cared achingly. That night I slept restlessly and trudged downstairs the next morning in very poor spirits.

Edward greeted me jauntily from the oval table as I walked into the breakfast room. "Good morning, Morninglory. This is the earliest I've seen you up in a while."

"Yes, it's too bad, isn't it? I've become spoiled so quickly. In the country I was always up when the rooster crowed."

"Do you miss the country?" he asked kindly.

"Oh no." I paused in the act of filling my plate. "Well, yes, just a little. It's not that I'm not grateful," I added hastily, "because I do enjoy life in London."

"Yes, I understand. When you examine the glitter closely, you discover it isn't gold but the sparkle of frost on a winter street which melts to nothing but a film of dew."

"How poetic," I murmured as I seated myself beside him.

"Yes, isn't it? I must jot it down and pass it along to George Bridgewater. Now then, your horse is being shod this morning, so we can't ride. However, I have a full day at my disposal and nothing would please me better than to escort you on any errands you might have or take you sightseeing."

"That's very kind of you." Then, suspiciously, "Maryanne didn't force you into asking me, did she?"

He laughed. "Good heavens no. Is she playing matchmaker between us?"

"I'm afraid she is," I replied apologetically.

He chuckled. "She certainly is indomitable. I'd have thought Lord Stanton's sudden flight would have left her disconsolate, but she has shaken off her gloom and is able to help manage the lives of other people."

240

"It's true that she seems to have recovered rapidly from her setback with Lord Stanton. You don't suppose she still cares for him, do you?"

"I think the rate at which she has forgotten the man is a tribute to how little she actually cared for him to begin with. Unless I am fair and far out, she has already set her cap for Baron Remly, and she and Sarah are out now purchasing clothes to entice the poor man." He shook his head in mock sympathy for Baron Remley. "Now, you run along upstairs and get ready."

We set out half an hour later and had a most pleasant morning. I was able to put aside the melancholy that had set in after yesterday morning's ride as we strolled from shop to shop. Edward waited patiently while I deliberated for twenty minutes over which shade of pink ribbon to buy before he finally made the decision for me. When we arrived back at the house, arm in arm, laughing merrily, Lord Linton was just leaving.

"Hello, Edward, Victoria," he greeted us frostily.

I quickly disengaged my arm from Edward's.

"If you have a moment, Edward, I'd like to consult with you."

"Of course, Wes." Edward smiled at me before he started down the hall after his guest. "We'll have to go shopping again. I quite enjoyed it," he told me as he tweaked the narrow brim of my apricot hat.

"Are you coming?" Lord Linton called testily from the study door.

"Yes," Edward replied casually.

I wandered into the drawing room and sat down in a chair facing out the wide window. I was just in time to witness a rousing fight between an orange vendor and a fat woman selling flowers. They were overturning carts and thrashing about ludicrously when the constable arrived to the dismay of onlookers and participants alike.

"Miss Lyons," the butler said in a voice that indicated it was his second or third attempt to gain my attention.

"Yes?" I asked, turning hastily to him.

"You have a visitor, a Sir Robert Lyonson."

I sprang from the chair and ran forward to throw my arms around Papa as he entered the room wearing a colorful if shabby waistcoat and trousers. He held me off with dignity. "Now, m' dear, ye must act with more becomin'ness."

"Papa," I admonished when the door closed behind the butler, "you're not a 'sir,' and your name isn't Lyonson, it's Lyons."

"Now, Vicky Ann, ain't no harm in addin' a title to make people think they're bein' visited by somebody what's important. And you might say I am a Lyonson because that was my father's name too."

"I'm so glad you came," I gurgled. "How's your leg?"

"Good. Real good. Lucky it was the one I already had the limp in."

"Does it hurt?"

"Off and on."

"But I almost forgot the good news. You're not wanted for murder anymore!"

"That's what I heered. Good thing too. It ain't proper for a minister of the Lord to be a wanted killer. Folks don't have as much faith in ye."

242

The door opened and Lord Linton entered. "I'm sorry to interrupt," he apologized, "but I wanted to meet you, sir, before you left. If you're not too busy, I have something I'd like to discuss with you."

"Be right pleased to, lad. Vicky Ann, why don't ye run along. This gentleman and me's got somethin' to deescuss."

"Of course, Papa." Lord Linton held the door for me.

He and Papa were closeted together for over an hour. I waited outside in the foyer on a straight-backed chair. It was becoming intolerably uncomfortable, but I was afraid to leave for fear Papa would vanish.

The drawing room door finally opened and Papa and the marquis emerged, chatting companionably. "I'll tell Sarah that you're here and see about having some tea served," Lord Linton said.

"Mighty kind of ye," Papa answered.

The marquis departed and returned a moment later with Sarah. He introduced her formally and Papa bowed over her hand with exaggerated gallantry. "I'm glad to meet them that's been takin' care of Vicky Ann."

Sarah responded politely, "You must be absolutely ravenous."

"Oh no, not a bit of it," Papa declaimed. "Howsom-ever I am hungry if ye have a bite to eat about."

"Of course, follow me. I believe we can have a luncheon served in the breakfast parlor without too much delay."

Papa fell into step behind Sarah and I jumped up to follow when Lord Linton took my arm and drew me into the drawing room. "One moment. I have something I wish to tell you." He indicated a chair and I sat. "Your father and I have decided that it would be well for him to remove to Meadowacres and take up residence in the gamekeeper's cottage. It's been vacant a year since my new gamekeeper has his own house, but it's in tolerably good shape and he would be close for you to visit whenever you go to Meadowacres."

"Papa will be living at Meadowacres?"

"Yes, he seemed to like the idea."

"I wish I could go with him," I said wistfully.

Lord Linton looked taken aback. "But what about your life here? Your friends and the balls? Surely you don't wish to leave all this?"

"I would miss it," I admitted, "but I could come back and visit with Sarah and Maryanne every now and again and they could visit me. It's been so long since I've had Papa to myself that I want to settle down quietly and live with him." My eyes filled with tears as I made my plea.

"I've had several offers for your hand, you know. If you wanted to, you could marry and live here in London."

"I want to go with Papa."

"If that's your choice, Victoria, then, of course, you may return with your father." He turned quickly to look out the window.

"Thank you, milord," I cried gratefully as I jumped up to run to the breakfast room to tell Papa.

I found him seated at the oval table with a large white napkin tucked under his chin and enough food before him to feed a family of four. Sarah excused herself to have a room put in order for Papa.

"I'm going with you," I said excitedly, dropping into Sarah's chair. "When are you leaving?"

"Tomorrow. Wesley is goin' to take me back in his carriage and git me settled in." He wiped a smear of jelly off his chin, then grinned mischieviously at me. "It'll be like old times abein' together, won't it, Vicky Ann?"

"Yes, Papa, it will," I responded enthusiastically.

CHAPTER TWENTY-FIVE

The next morning Lord Linton arrived for us early. Maryanne sniffled her disappointment at losing me and made last-minute entreaties for me to stay as Papa stuffed some of the breakfast biscuits into his coat pocket and thanked Sarah very kindly for having us. He graciously invited her to drop in at the manor house if she were ever near Meadowacres.

Inside the carriage Papa attempted to strike up a conversation with Lord Linton, but it was more like a monologue as the marquis had very little to say. Papa changed tactics and switched to asking questions. His lordship answered politely but showed no inclination to extend the discussion. Finally, turning to the religious front, Papa asked if Lord Linton had found his salvation.

"I believe I have," he replied slowly, looking at me quizzically.

Thus encouraged, Papa launched into an oratory on the evils of sin. We arrived at Meadowacres many moral lessons and platitudes later, following a night spent at an inn where Papa had to keep to his room because he feared the landlord would recognize him from a previous trip through.

The gamekeeper's cottage had been fixed up prettily with blue-checked curtains, new whitewash, and a well-scrubbed kitchen. Mrs. Worthing displayed it to me proudly as Papa looked through the cottage with the delight of a child at Christmas. He exclaimed over the pump that didn't have to be primed and thoroughly examined the cow that had been provided.

The next day he walked around the neighborhood, acquainting himself with the sights and people. When he came back in the evening, he moved from his tick mattress bed to a hedgerow behind the house, insisting he could sleep more comfortably there.

Oddly enough Lord Linton did not return to London but announced that he was taking up permanent residence at Meadowacres. I had all this from Mrs. Worthing because, of course, the marquis did not come to the cottage.

The third day of our sojourn Edward appeared at the cottage door. "I'm here visiting Wes and he's too busy to talk with me. I thought we could go for a ride about the country. I've brought along a gentle mare."

"How about a walk?" I bargained.

"A walk it is," he laughed. "I have news of interest—Sarah is to be married."

I stopped in the act of wrapping a shawl about my shoulders. "Sarah! To whom?"

"Sir Thurston. Maryanne is disconsolate. She said it was a lame trick, no joke intended, for him to come limping up to the house pretending to court her when he was really interested in Sarah. She seems to have forgotten she would have no part of him at the time, preferring the long-gone Lord Stanton."

"When is the wedding to be?"

"Some time next month." He took my arm and we strolled about the lanes and woods for over an hour discussing this interesting development. When we reached the back door of the cottage, he bowed and left. I entered through the back just as Papa was walking out of the front door with a bag over his shoulder.

"I guess I'll be leaving now, Vicky Ann," he said as casually as if he were going out to milk the cow.

I smiled my understanding. "I'll see you the next time you're through, Papa."

He grinned happily and started down the lane. I watched him go with a tinge of sadness, but I knew the walls of the cottage had already begun to close in on him. He would be happier roaming. He turned and waved and I waved back.

Late the next evening while I was churning butter, Lord Linton burst into the cottage. I was startled. He hadn't even knocked. "Mrs. Worthing tells me that your father is gone. Is that true?" he demanded.

"Yes," I replied calmly as I continued churning.

He paced the floor. "God, the whole place is mad!" He uttered a strong expletive. "Am I to be the only one around here who is sane? Your father just ups and leaves, and you don't have the good sense to tell me you are without protection."

"Why do I need protection here on your land?" I asked, looking up curiously.

"Because you are living on an isolated part of my land for one thing. For another, did it never occur to you that you might need protection from me?"

"Not for a long time," I answered honestly.

My answer seemed to exasperate him. "Pack your things," he ordered curtly. "You're coming back to the manor house with me."

It seemed easier to placate him tonight and talk reason with him in the morning, so I packed a few things and followed him out the door. I had expected a coach, but there was only his horse. Without a word he lifted me up and threw me into the saddle, mounted behind me, and headed for the house.

At the house Mrs. Worthing greeted me in surprise as the marquis instructed her to show me up to a bedroom. She led me up to a large green room, whispering to me excitedly, "Lord Linton is going to be married."

"Oh." I could frame no other reply. A familiar dull ache in my stomach began to throb. So Clarissa had persuaded him after all, I thought dejectedly.

Oblivious to my torment, Mrs. Worthing continued, "Yes, he told me himself the other day. He wants to have the house prepared for his new bride by the first of next month. Gracious, that's only three weeks away! Think of the people who'll be coming here! It will be something to behold."

"Indeed it will," I returned faintly.

Carried away on the wave of her own enthusiasm, Mrs. Worthing didn't notice my lack of it. She continued regaling me with her pleasure at seeing his lordship settled down to wedded bliss. I interrupted her, pleading a headache, and she left, prescribing rest.

At that exact moment I felt that I would never again get a good night's rest. It wasn't that I cared if he married, it was just that, well . . . Well I was *not* jealous. I repeated these statements emphatically to myself over the next four hours. By one o'clock I began to realize that it was hopeless. I wouldn't have been crying so hard if I didn't care. It was no use trying to sleep. I threw a peignor over my nightdress and crept downstairs to the library. Perhaps I could read myself to sleep.

I pulled a book off the shelf and opened the cover. "Wesley, his book" was scrawled inside the flyleaf in a boyish hand. I smiled tremulously, thinking of the marquis as a prankster schoolboy with a wicked gleam in those devastating green eyes. My smile broke over into a sob. I felt someone put their arms around me and pull me to them. I opened my eyes to look straight into a snowy white cravat which I was washing down with a flood of tears. I sniffled for a full two minutes before I could master myself enough to look up. When I did, Lord Lynley was smiling whimsically down at me. I tried to smile back.

"Pretty Victoria, with your so black hair and your so blue eyes in your so beautiful face," Edward murmured. "I wish it were me."

From the doorway a voice broke in. "Edward, why are you having an assignation at this hour of the night in a secluded room of my house with Miss Lyons?"

Edward winked at me, released me, and turned to Lord Linton. "My pardon, Wes. I was on my way to the kitchen when I happened into the library. You're a lucky man. I had my hopes there for a while, but I soon saw how the land lay." He smiled at each of us. "I'll continue on to the kitchen," he announced and left.

I stared at the floor. Lord Linton crossed the room and stood in front of me. "Well?" he drawled.

I stood mute, not daring to look at him for fear of betraying myself.

"It seems the least you could do is reward me with the same welcome you gave Edward."

I blushed scarlet and tried to stammer an explanation.

"Save it," he whispered as he crushed his lips down on mine. He kissed me tenderly and at length. I returned his kiss unreservedly. Finally he drew back and looked searchingly into my face. I blinked to clear my head. He laughed softly and kissed my flushed cheek. "I said three weeks, but I don't know . . ." His voice was muffled in my hair.

I drew away from him. "Three weeks before you marry?" I accused. "How can you stand here kissing me?"

"I intend to continue kissing you," he said unrepentantly.

"Even after you're married?" I asked in a husky voice.

"Yes," he replied steadily, "especially then. In fact, I shall probably do far more than kiss you."

My cheeks flamed and I tore myself away from the hands he was bringing around me. "You, sir, are an incorrigible rake!" I shouted at him.

"Yes," he smiled. "But there is no need to shout it at this hour. The servants are already well aware of it. Why don't we sit down?" he asked blandly.

I stared at him in disbelief. He had no sense of wrong; he had no scruples. But I must have even less because I stayed. I sank down on the settee and he sat beside me.

"Victoria," he clasped my hand. "My first encounter

with you was to nearly run you over. After that I made several inexcusable attempts on your virtue and from there we progressed to being cordial enemies. Do you not feel it is time to alter the course of our relationship?"

"I don't know what you mean—" I began falteringly, looking about the room in an effort to avoid looking at Lord Linton.

"Well, since we have spent so much time being at odds with each other, is it not time we were friends? After all, look at the terms you are on with Edward, and you don't know him nearly as well as you do me. He has always been at pains to show you his good side, but you have seen all sides of me."

"I am not on any terms with Edward," I sputtered.

"You were in his arms when I came in," he replied evenly.

"That was because I was upset."

"About what?" he fired at me.

I shrugged dejectedly. "It doesn't matter."

"Victoria, you will be stubborn to the last, will you not?"

I looked at him in confusion.

"I am going to marry you and that is final. If you cannot bring yourself to say you love me madly, then at least smile sweetly and melt into my arms."

My eyes opened wide. I moved my lips but no words came out. "You want to marry me?" I finally choked out.

"I intend to marry you," he stated firmly. Suddenly he smiled a smile that lit his whole face and he bent to kiss me. "Don't say anything yet," he commanded.

My head was beginning to swim from the wonder of

it all. He really intended to marry me! I did melt into his arms then, and it was a good quarter of an hour before he released me slowly.

"Will you marry me, Victoria?" I nodded vigorously. He drew back and regarded me. "Are you certain, Victoria?" I nodded even more emphatically and leaned forward with my eyes closed and my mouth pursed for another kiss. "It was just as I suspected. You did throw yourself at Edward."

I opened my eyes but my protest died in my throat as I saw his gently mocking eyes. They softened as I gazed into them and then our lips met again.

"I don't want to break anything up, but if you two continue much longer in this manner, it will be necessary for the marriage to be moved up considerably," Edward interrupted from the doorway.

Lord Linton did not look up from my face. "I wish that fellow would go to the devil," he stated conversationally.

"I'm sure you do, but someone has to look after this young lady's virtue," Edward replied in amused and matter-of-fact tones.

The marquis shook his head slightly and moved back. "I regret to admit that he is right. Go to bed, sweet. We will discuss this in the morning."

I went. But it was fated to be a sleepless night and I was in the breakfast room at six in the morning demanding that Janey assume her responsibility as maid and wake up Lord Linton. When she refused adamantly, I boldly took myself up to his room and knocked on the door. The valet opened the door with as much astonishment as it is possible for a man half-asleep to feel. "The house is surely afire, madame," he stated upon seeing me framed in the doorway.

"By no means," I bubbled. "I wish to see Lord Linton."

"His lordship is sleeping at this present moment. Perhaps if you were to wait for a few hours—"

"No, I'm up," Lord Linton interrupted, walking up to the door buttoning his shirt.

"Very good, sir," the valet said imperturbably, bowed, and left.

I smiled excitedly at the marquis.

"Yes, my dear?"

"You said we would talk this morning," I reminded him.

"Ah, so I did. Actually I didn't mean precisely at six o'clock. I rather thought we might wait and talk later. Would that be all right?"

My face fell. "Yes, of course, I only thought you might be anxious to talk."

He laughed and, threading his arm through mine, led me downstairs and out into the garden. Mrs. Worthing threw us a look of pure astonishment as we passed the kitchen window. I smiled and waved. We sat down on a stone bench and milord put both arms around me and pulled me close to him.

"Victoria, you have made me feel like a young and foolish man again. I never wanted to marry anyone until I met you, and I fought my feelings so hard that I made us both very miserable. That night in the study when you came to me so warmly and it was so natural, I knew that I was desperately in love with you. No woman had ever made me feel like that before."

"I didn't think you remembered," I said wonderingly. "I thought you were drunk."

"Are you serious?" He studied me in disbelief. "I was devilish drunk but I remember every detail."

"But why did you become so cold to me afterward?"

He smiled a sweet, sad smile. "I was afraid. Lord, I'd never felt anything that strong before. I was so afraid I'd lost control of my feelings that I hid behind that damned aloof attitude. It was stupid. Do you forgive me for that?"

I nodded.

"And now, my raven-haired beauty, I will move mountains for you, I will do anything in the world for you—save one. Do you want to know what that is?" He looked at me with tender amusement.

"Yes," I murmured, looking up into his face with reverence.

"I will never again leave my bed at six o'clock in the morning for you. From now on, any discussions you and I have at that hour will take place in bed and will involve very little talking. Do you understand?"

My response was lost as his mouth came down on mine.